THEIR CHILDREN WILL SEE
and Other Stories

THESE STORIES of the Gaelic-speaking communities
of the Western Isles of Scotland are all concerned
with the individual in society: individuals in communities under political, cultural and economic
pressures; communities compelled to adapt to major
changes in their circumstances, or struggling to
maintain their integrity and the continuity of their
traditions; individuals in societies threatened by
ideological and cultural dichotomies. Mr Grant
writes of the ties of place which transcend time,
distance and personal conflict.

Also by James Shaw Grant

HIGHLAND VILLAGES

THEIR CHILDREN WILL SEE

and Other Stories

JAMES SHAW GRANT

ROBERT HALE · LONDON

ISBN 0 7091 7311 3

Robert Hale Limited
Clerkenwell House
Clerkenwell Green
London, EC1R 0HT

Printed in Great Britain by
Clarke, Doble & Brendon Ltd.
Plymouth and London

Contents

1 Their Children Will See   9

2 Lament for Ensay   31

3 Blossom   75

4 Requiem for Seonaid   88

5 Jonah on Rousay   118

6 Fiddler in Hell   150

ACKNOWLEDGEMENT

The first story in this collection, "Their Children Will See", previously appeared in "Brunton's Miscellany" under the title "Clann nan Doill", to the Editor of which the author wishes to express his thanks.

For James B. Caird

Their Children Will See

I don't think I ever told you how the people of Ardvasar, on the Atlantic coast of the Hebrides, came to be known as Clann nan Doill—"the children of the blind". It is an interesting story, which I pieced together from local tradition, checked carefully against known historical facts.

Ardvasar is an unlikely place for anyone to live, especially anyone who is blind or even near-sighted. It is one of those unprepossessing hillsides which would never have been occupied at all if people had not been driven there by sheer necessity during the years of rapidly rising population in the Hebrides when hunger pressed against the means of subsistence with a starkness which would have delighted Malthus, and which created social problems complex enough to have baffled a saint—not that there were many saints around.

The houses were perched on the summit of a gently rising plateau which terminated abruptly just behind them with a sheer drop of more than two hundred feet to the sea. On one side there was a declivity almost as sheer, down the side of which a zigzag path had been scratched, or just worn by many feet, giving access to a boulder beach in a little cove from which fishing boats could be launched in calm weather, which was not very frequent, and where, by the united strength of all the men and women in the village, they could be hauled up to the top of the bank, above high water mark, when they returned from a fishing expedition, if they did return.

The houses had almost no shelter from the incessant Atlantic gales, and, although they cowered into the little lee they could find where the plateau began to drop towards the beach, only the earliest settlers had even this degree of shelter as each new house, built as the population grew, was thrust more nakedly into the wind.

The one good feature of the site was that the extreme exposure had prevented the formation of deep peat, and the wind, rain and ice of many centuries had eroded sufficient of the cliff top to produce a thin mineral soil from which grudging crops could be raised with the aid of manure and smoke-saturated thatch from the houses, which the cattle shared with the humans in their mutual struggle for conservation and survival. They also used seaweed from the beach below, dragged laboriously up the cliff path by the women in creels.

It was from the farmer at Crogorm, in the sheltered valley at the foot of the plateau, the people of Ardvasar first learned that they were to be evicted—and the message came to them in a typically brutal way.

Some of the crofters' stock had trespassed on the farm. The farmer impounded them and sent for the owners. It was a regular occurrence. The crofters did what they could to keep the stock from straying, but it was not easy: with the green fields before them and the wind at their backs, the beasts could not be restrained and, although the crofters built a wall between them and the farm, the only material they had were the rounded boulders from the beach, which rocked and chattered in a gale, and could be breasted aside like water by a hungry bullock. Lugging huge lumps of stone to the cliff top with their naked hands, in numbers sufficient to make a mile-long dyke was a labour as onerous for the crofters as building the Pyramids, and as frustrating as the labour of Sisyphus. They had done their best but the problem still remained.

When the summons from the farmer came, as it did from time to time, the unhappy crofters went meekly and paid their fine, and drove their bullocks home again, hoping that next time it might be a neighbour who got his fingers burnt because, although they all kept a little money for such eventualities, they could not afford to bail their animals out very often.

On this occasion, the culprits, or the victims, were aghast when the farmer demanded twice the usual ransom. They protested bitterly, but he was quite unmoved. "If you don't want your beasts, I'll just keep them," he said. "I'll have grazing for them in the spring. By that time, you lazy buggers will be out of here. You'll work for your breakfast then! The place you're going to is mighty cold."

They pressed him for information, but he just laughed. "You'll be told time enough," he said. "It won't take long to organise the flitting. It would be simpler to put a match to everything, and even at that it would be a bloody poor bonfire."

Beyond that, they could get nothing from him. They paid their double fines, and drove the skinny beasts back up the hill, brooding as they went on the farmer's threat.

It is difficult for us to understand why anyone should be

reluctant to leave a countryside as hard and impoverished as Ardvasar, especially a seafaring people who took their living from the Western Ocean, and in whose veins ran the blood of great adventurers like the Vikings and Celts, and possibly also of the Phoenicians, and whose oral tradition still carried the dying echoes of the culture brought to them by Irish missionaries, whose cockle-shell boats penetrated to remote outposts like the Flannans and Rona, and even to America itself.

The explanation can be found on the beach below the village, round the tide-mark on the rocks. The lobsters and crabs which live in the depths of the ocean scurry here and there in search of food, and the birds which nest at the top of the cliff roam the hemisphere as the seasons change, but the shell-backed creatures which live where sea and land contend, cling grimly to the rocks: they must, to survive. Although there was no physical link, the people of Ardvasar were attached to their little hovels, and their coffin-shaped feannags, and their half-starved cattle, with the tenacity of the limpet, and for precisely the same reason: to resist the wash and suck of a hostile ebb. Every change their lives had known until then had been a change for the worse: they felt like a man who has been blindfolded and driven to walk the plank, each reluctant footstep taking him further from the safety of the ship and nearer the moment when he must plunge into the void.

Desperation can drive a community to migrate, but until the ultimate point of desperation is reached, all the energy of mind and body is directed to resisting the need for change, so that the moment of greatest immobility is the moment before the dam bursts, and the flood goes roaring free.

Late into the night, the people of Ardvasar sat around their peat fires discussing the threat which was hanging over them. Was the farmer bluffing? Had the Factor told him something? Was the decision unalterable? Where were they being sent? When would they know? Who would tell them? How would they go? Would anyone lead them? Could they do anything to avert the calamity? The answers they arrived at were as insubstantial and took as many changing shapes as the blue smoke rising from the hearth, which disappeared in the darkness above their heads. At last they went to bed and slept uneasily until they were awakened by the excited shouts of the herd boy they had sent to keep a watch on the wall at dawn, in case the cattle strayed again.

"The redcoats are coming! The redcoats are coming!"

Men and women tumbled out of bed and stood in doorways in their shirts and shifts, with hands cupped over their eyes against the morning sun as they adjusted to the brightness after the gloom of the windowless interior.

Away in the distance, from the north, from the direction of the town, they could see a line of figures moving slowly across the moor, and now and then they saw, or thought they saw, a flash of colour and the glint of steel.

"Get me the glass," shouted Murchadh Ban, who was known far beyond his native village as a bard and who, among the older folk, had the reputation of being something even more.

The glass was a ship's telescope which he had retrieved many years before from a wreck, and in superstitious minds there was no clear distinction between the tube through which Murchadh could see events at a distance in space and the stone, pierced by a hole, which was given to Coinneach

13

Odhar, the legendary seer by the disembodied wraith of a Norwegian princess, and through which he could look on events still distant in time. If they had been Catholics, they would have crossed themselves whenever the telescope was exhibited in their presence, and perhaps some of them did, because the Presbyterian revivalism of the nineteenth century had not yet caught up with them and what little religion they had was a confused mixture of many elements, dating back to the old Celtic church and even beyond. In any event, most of them kept a respectful distance as Murdo steadied the telescope against the gable of his house.

"They are redcoats, and they aren't," he said cryptically, and took another long look.

"Here, Duncan, what do you make of it?" he said at last, handing the glass to the man who was without question the best skipper in the village: a man who was fearless in a boat but never took undue risks, because he could see a storm approaching before there was a cloud in the sky, just as he could read the signs of fish from the surface of the water although the shoals were hidden in the darkness far below.

"These men are tied together with a rope," said Duncan at last. It was characteristic of him that he uttered a plain statement without any attempt to interpret a phenomenon he did not understand, unlike his neighbours who were always readier with their explanations than their facts.

There was an excited buzz of conversation. They were relieved to know that this was obviously not the Factor marching on the village with redcoats to fire the thatch, but what was the meaning of Murdo's cryptic ambiguity, and Duncan's even stranger fact?

"Pressed men," said an anxious whisper, and many of the

14

youths began hurriedly to dress in case they had to take to the hills.

"They're not pressed men," said Murdo.

"There's only one man with them, and he has no gun. He is walking in front instead of at the rear: they can't be prisoners," said Duncan, supplying the essential facts on which Murchadh Ban's opinion was founded, even if he had not observed them all, or noted them with Duncan's clarity.

For a good half-hour they watched the procession moving slowly and uncertainly across the moor. Because of the boggy moor, they had to make long detours like a ship tacking towards port against a contrary wind, but they were also hampered by the rope which restrained their movement, and by something else. It was Murdo who got the explanation first, his intuition again carrying him further in a poet's leap than the known facts might warrant.

"These men are blind," he said sharply, putting down the glass.

"There's one man leading them," said Duncan, taking the glass from him. "The men immediately behind him are walking with some confidence, but those at the end of the rope are slipping and slithering and falling in the bogs."

"We must go to help them," he added with decision.

He was still as far as any of them from an explanation of the mystery but he had clearly decided that here was no threat to the villagers, but neighbours (in the Biblical sense) whose need was greater than theirs.

Relieved of their immediate anxiety, and glad to have something positive to do, the crowd raced down the hillside, men and women alike in an excited mob, led by the young men who a few moments earlier had been preparing to take to the hills for fear of the press gang.

"Are you sure it's not a trick?" said Alasdair Cam to Duncan, as they followed the others at a more sedate pace suited to their years and their dignity as skippers of fishing boats. The epithet "cam", or twisted, was conferred on the progenitor of the Campbells and the progenitor of the Camerons for physical reasons, but it was given to Alasdair because he had a tortuous mind and saw a sinister intent in every action of a neighbour, even of his closest friend.

Duncan made no reply. He was reasonably certain that what he had seen through the glass was a group of blind men being led across broken country by a single guide who had roped them together to make his task manageable. But he was puzzled to think who the blind men could be, and puzzled even more by the feeling that he knew their guide. They were too far away for him to see the features clearly, even with the glass, but Duncan felt there was something in the man's gait which was familiar.

The explanation came from Murchadh Ban who had gone on ahead to a point of vantage and was now having a closer look at the little procession through his glass. As Duncan and Alasdair reached him, he leapt to his feet shouting, "Duncan! Duncan! I have seen a ghost. The man who is leading the blind is your own blood brother."

And Duncan knew. Without taking the glass again. He had last seen Norman as a stripling of 17, taking the King's Shilling from his Chief at the Drum Head, not far from the spot where they were standing. Now he was a mature man in his thirties, tanned by the suns of Italy, Egypt, India and Java, bearded and in uniform, or at least in the remnants of a uniform, leading back to their homes more than a dozen of

16

his comrades, blinded by ophthalmia when they fought the Turks.

Duncan took the glass again, and lay in the heather to steady his arm. He didn't look at Norman this time—he knew that Murchadh had identified him correctly, but he scrutinised the others one by one, trying to roll back the years and recognise the youths he had known in Ardvasar and the villages round about, from which three hundred men had gone on the same day at their Chief's behest to fight Napoleon.

"Neil is there as well," he said when he got to his feet. "He's the last man in the line, but at least he's alive, thank God."

"How like Neil to take the worst berth, and how like Norman to show no favour to his brother," said Murchadh. "They are still their father's sons, and it's good to have them back."

Duncan was pleased by the compliment to his brothers and his father and, by implication, to himself, but his response was the gruff comment, "More mouths to feed. A blind man can't use a spade or reef a sail."

"That's a harsh thing to say," commented Murchadh in some surprise.

"It's easier for me to say it seeing my own brothers are there," said Duncan. "It is something we have to reckon with."

By this time the young men had reached the strangers, but had no idea who they were. Ragged and dirty after ploughtering through the bogs, they might have been ship-wrecked seamen or tinkers, but for the odd bits of uniform they wore. Then they spoke. In Gaelic. Ardvasar Gaelic.

Although some of them used an admixture of English words.

There was a general hubbub by the time Duncan and the older men arrived. Each of the soldiers had a group of youngsters round him answering avid questions about fathers and mothers, sweethearts, friends, brothers and sisters, of whom they had heard nothing for more than a decade.

Duncan walked straight across to Norman and took his hand. The brothers looked at each other and smiled. Neither spoke, but together they walked across to Neil. "It's Duncan," said Norman. When Neil felt his brother's hand in his he squeezed it warmly and, still holding it, passed his free hand along Duncan's arm and shoulder and across his head, then gently over his face, as if reassuring himself.

"Where am I?" he asked at length.

"Just where you were when I saw you last," said Duncan, "by the fank where we were shearing when the Chief came to take two men from every family for the wars."

"I was looking straight at Scalpay when I took the shilling," said Neil. "And there were two boats fishing in the sound. One of them had a small white patch like a cross on its brown sail. I remember wondering which of the villages it came from because I had never seen it before. Stand me as I was then."

Duncan took him gently by the arm and turned him so that he was facing Scalpay. Neil raised his arm and pointed at the island just as if he could see it. Then he named all the islands one by one, turning slowly as he spoke so that he pointed precisely at each in turn and, when his arm at length was pointing to the coast of the main island on which he stood, he named the headlands and the hills, a litany of names that was almost a poem—and every name rich in

18

associations, not only from their own personal experience but from the communal experience of their people, accumulated over the centuries and growing more precious with the passage of time, so that events which had happened hundreds of years ago were as vivid as those of last week.

"Now," he said, "I should be pointing at my mother's house. Is she at the door to greet me?"

"No," said Duncan. "She's here"—and the crowd moved back to make way for an old woman doubled over her stick who stumbled forward to embrace him.

"You didn't think I would come back to look after you in your old age," said Neil. "No one will want to marry me now—unless some ugly cow that couldn't get a man with eyes in his head. But I have money in my purse, more than ever I had before. Although I can't see the colour of it, I can hear it sing." He took out a fistful of coins as he spoke and jingled them gaily. "You'll want for nothing now."

Then, almost as if he sensed Duncan's unspoken question, and knew of the fears he had confided to Murchadh, he said, "We have all got a pension from the King for our eyes, and another pension for a boy to lead us about."

Murchadh looked at Duncan and winked. "I would give my own eyes," he said, "for a pocketful like that."

By this time Norman had untied the men he was guiding and, taking command of the young men as one accustomed to some authority, he assigned them in groups to lead the blind men home. Many of the blind men came from villages further up the parish than Ardvasar, and some of them had many miles still to go, but now each had a convoy of eager helpers, who took him by the arm, and carried him over the rougher ground. Duncan and Norman took Neil between

19

them, walking slowly so that their mother could keep pace with them. The two other blind men who belonged to Ardvasar had also been claimed by relations and were now being hurried home.

No one in the parish went to bed that night. In every village young and old gathered in the homes to which the blind soldiers had gone. They laughed and they sang. They drank the home-brewed ale which was their common drink and the whisky illicitly distilled in caves and mountain bothies which was reserved for special occasions. But some of the blind men asked instead for buttermilk, which they had not tasted since they last slaked their thirst at the scything.

"Many a thirst I have had since then, and what would I have given for a drink of this," said Neil as he raised a rough clay jug of buttermilk before his sightless eyes.

There was never a night of so much merriment in Ardvasar before, not even if all the weddings the oldest of them could remember were rolled together into one great spree. Some of the blind men even tried to dance a few steps with the girls who had been their sweethearts but who were now prematurely aged by toil, and married to other men with children of their own not far from marriageable age.

But, for the most part, they just talked. About old days and old friends. The blind men brought news of their comrades who were still in arms. They were able to tell the villagers who had been killed and how they had died, and who had still been alive when they were last with the regiment, and they bared their arms to show the children their own innumerable scars.

Tears of sorrow and tears of joy flowed together in the

darkness and even those who were weeping for their own misfortune rejoiced in the homecoming of their neighbours.

"That is something I never thought I would live to see," said Murchadh, as his brother's widow, who had been a notable singer in her youth, was coaxed by the blind men to sing a favourite song. She was still in mourning for her husband who was lost at sea with two companions, and a few minutes earlier she had learned that her young brother had been run through by an Indian lance at the Battle of Assaye. Years had passed since his death, but for her it had just occurred. She was sobbing in the shadows when her name was called. Murchadh and Duncan tried to hush the blind men, but by this time some of them had drunk so much they couldn't be stopped, and she hadn't the heart to say them 'no'. She refused to come forward into the light of the fire, but sitting where she was she sang an old lament with a heartbreak that was new.

There were no shouts of "tha i math" when she had finished, no calls for more; even the ale and the whisky were silenced by the searing splendour of her song, and they all sat looking into their own memories silently, as faces and figures from the past took shape for them in the glowing embers on the hearth.

When talk was resumed it was subdued for a time, but the restraint soon wore off again, and the laughter and rousing choruses were less inhibited than ever.

Night after night the ceilidh went on. As soon as it was dark the whole village gathered into one or two favourite houses. All the songs and tales and reminiscences in the great storehouse of communal memory were called for, and a new dimension was added to the folklore of the village as the blind men told of their own adventures in the cold of Flanders where brandy froze in the bottles, and the heat of the desert where men died in the sun; of battles and sieges and long route marches, voyages in crowded troop ships, great towns with more people than they had thought were in the world, and buildings as high as the cliffs where they used to go nesting; eastern bazaars and palaces and treasure, warriors and princes they had captured, and dark-skinned men of various shades who spoke outlandish languages of which they brought some fragments back to adorn their stories, giving them the ring of truth.

But all the stories of conquest and of death were eclipsed by their account of their comrades who were captured by the Turks, then marched between two lines of severed heads on Turkish lances, to the Cairo market where they were sold as slaves.

That was almost the only note of bitterness in their Odyssey. Death was clean and it was unavoidable and they took it as it came, but everything in their ancestry and traditions, their love of freedom and instinctive human dignity was revolted by what they had heard of the comrades who were sold into slavery.

The stories were told in their own tongue about men they all knew; it was almost as if only the people of Ardvasar had gone to the war, and by their own unaided strength won victories greater than those of Cu Chulainn, in lands so distant that even the Vikings had never seen them, establishing an empire greater than Charlemagne or even Alexander, although none of them had heard of Charlemagne or Alexander, to give scale to their achievement, and even the King for whom they annexed these territories was a remote figure

22

of whom they knew only by hearsay, as they knew of Cu Chulainn himself, and who did not even speak their language, or know of their existence.

It was on the fourth morning when they were all sleeping late after successive nights of revelry, and the sun was well up in the sky, that the Factor came with the message from their Chief, the same Chief who had enlisted them to fight for King and country, that he had no more use for them, but, as a generous gesture, was prepared to pay the cost of shipping them all to America.

"He needs the land," said the Factor bluntly. "The farmer at Crogorm is offering a bigger rent than you can pay. And he will pay in cash instead of fish and skins and feathers."

"You will be well off in the New World," he added. "There's game on the hills and fish in the rivers. No laws about poaching! You can live like lords with the Indians to fetch and carry."

They all looked at him sullenly and said nothing, but the Factor was in a jocular mood and would not be stopped. "Think of the rent you'll save when you haven't got me to worry you. And the shelter you'll have in the forests compared with this bleak hill. Man, I would leave the crowd of you here and go myself, if the Chief could spare me."

In spite of the light-hearted approach, he had made his arrangements carefully. The Sheriff Officer was with him, and witnesses to see that formal notices of removal were served on each of them, and little handbills were posted up in English and Gaelic to tell them when and where to join the vessel on which they were to sail.

Fear of the unknown, anger at being treated like cattle driven to market, dismay at their betrayal by the Chief they had served so well, swept through the village. They were used to obeying a leader, and had come to expect fair dealing from those who led them. That had been true of their chiefs in the past, and it had certainly been true of their officers in the army: they might be harsh but the men respected them. But now they were at a loss, floundering about like a rudderless vessel tossed this way and that in a broken sea.

There was a great deal of hot-headed talk by the men and weeping by the women, and even those who kept their heads found it difficult to frame a course of action. The three brothers so recently reunited, and normally so placid, quarrelled bitterly until at last their frail old mother ordered them out of the house and told them not to return until the fresh air had cooled them.

It was Duncan who started the row. In his direct way, he said what he thought without troubling to prepare other people for ideas he had lived with for a long time in the secrecy of his own mind.

"I hate the little rat," he said emphatically, as the Factor left them. "But what he says is true. The sooner we go the better."

Norman rounded on him. "Every day for the past ten years, every hour and every minute, I have looked forward to coming home. Now that I am home, I am staying home."

"I can't see you growing fat on what you'll get to eat here," said Duncan.

"Look, brother," said Norman, "I have seen countries you've never even heard of. I have seen wealth that would astonish you: gold and jewels heaped on a palace floor like potatoes in a barn. But I have also seen poverty. I have seen

24

men and women and children so thin. . . ." He paused for a moment looking for a simile, and then, trying to take the heat out of the discussion, added with a smile, "They were thinner than Pharaoh's lean kine, and they were so thin you could only see them in a dream."

"You can see poverty here too, and it's no dream," growled Duncan.

"We may be poor," retorted Norman, "but there are others poorer in any country you care to go to. I've had my fill of wandering and I'm staying here."

"Yes," said Duncan, "that's the trouble. You see things as a man who's just come home, with the taste of the fatted calf still on his lips. You've had your fill of wandering, but I've had my fill of Ardvasar."

"What's wrong with Ardvasar?" snapped Norman.

"There's plenty right with it," said Duncan, with a vain attempt at appeasement. "But you must face the facts. The older villages in the parish—Broadford, Dervaig, Cornaig-more—they all have machair for the potatoes, and green hills at the sheiling, and safe harbours where you can work a boat. But this is just a hard knuckle of land and a death trap for fishermen. If you had the pick of the parish would you choose Ardvasar?"

"I haven't the pick of the parish," retorted Norman, "but I was born in Ardvasar, I fought for Ardvasar, and I'll live in Ardvasar until they carry me down to the graveyard. I'll have all the machair then that I need."

"It may be sooner than you think," said Duncan. "Tell me, have you a boat?"

"No," said Norman, adding pointedly, "but my brother Duncan has."

"Right," said Duncan. "I give you a berth. Who do I turn away to make room for you, Domhnull Ian or Snowy?"

"Damn you!" said Norman, and it was then their mother told them to go. Norman knew that Duncan could only accommodate him by displacing someone else and, even if the others were not brothers, they were friends and neighbours who had worked with him well.

They said nothing for a few minutes after they went out. The fact that they had to guide Neil brought them together and eased the tension. He had taken no part in the conversation, but he was listening intently.

As they stood there, Neil drew a deep breath. "I think," he said, "I'm looking towards the hills. There's heather in the air, and I can feel the sun on my face."

"Yes," said Duncan. "You are looking at the hills we will never forget, whether we are looking on them with our eyes like Norman and myself or seeing them in the mind like you. I dare say, Neil, you're seeing them clearer than we are because you're still seeing them with the eyes of a barefoot boy."

"Norman," he added after a pause, "it won't do for us to quarrel. Too many people will look to us for guidance. It seems to me there are three courses open to us. I would like you to tell me which you advise. We can take the Factor's offer and go to America. We can drift off to the Lowlands in ones and twos to find what work we can in the towns. Or we can stay here and fight it out when the Factor comes with the redcoats."

Norman was sobered by Duncan's quiet enumeration of the choices and he replied with great deliberation, "I've seen more fighting in my day than most people, and I'm afraid

26

of no man that ever breathed. But we have no weapons, and even if we had, no one could defend this open hillside. Only the young can go to the towns, and they'll go as strays, separated from the flock until there's no flock left. If we go to America we can go together and take our language and our customs with us."

Duncan put his hand on Norman's shoulder. "It's a hard choice, but it's the only one." Neil said nothing.

Once he had been convinced that they must go, Norman became the organiser of the whole expedition. He backed Duncan up in the argument which raged through the village. He dealt in a blunt soldierlike way with Alasdair Cam, who went round the houses whispering that Duncan was in the Factor's pay. He made light of the difficulties of settling in a new country and the dangers of the voyage, drawing on his own past experience to encourage the faint-hearted. In a short time, the people of Ardvasar were almost looking forward to the adventure, although still filled with the 'cianalas' which so distinguishes the Gael.

What really won them round was Norman's revenge on the farmer. "Look," he said, "if we don't sell them until the ship is ready to sail, we'll have to give our cattle away. Let's fatten them first and choose our market."

"What will you fatten them on—air?" asked Murchadh Ban, looking at the hill where hardly a blade of grass remained.

"It's an extraordinary thing," said Norman, "that we should send boys out every morning with stones to prevent the cattle from breaking down the wall, when just as easily we could go ourselves with sticks to prevent the farmer from poinding the cattle."

They laughed uproariously. That night great gaps appeared in the wall. In the morning, all the Ardvasar cattle and sheep were in the farmer's corn, eating as they had never eaten before, while the crofters lounged about with flails and bits of driftwood, and the farmer looked on helplessly, because he knew that before the law could intervene effectively, they would all be on the high seas.

By the time the vessel arrived, the stock had been fattened and disposed of, and what equipment and gear the villagers were taking with them had been packed for stowing under Norman's professional eye. But there was one unexpected difficulty—Neil and his two blind companions refused to sail.

Argument, exhortation, pleading were in vain, and finally Norman had to organise the strongest of the villagers into three groups to carry them bodily to the beach. The vessel was lying some distance off shore, and the emigrants were ferried out to her in open boats. The Emigration Agent and the Factor stood together on the beach, supervising the operation.

"What the hell is this?" demanded the Emigration Agent, when he saw three groups of struggling men approach.

"It's a small matter," said the Factor. "Just three old soldiers who have lost their sight. They don't want to leave home, but what does it matter to them?—they can't see where they are in any event."

"It doesn't matter to them, but it matters to me," said the Emigration Agent. "There's nothing about blind men in your bloody bargain. I stretched a point to cover the old folk and the children, but who the hell wants useless lumber on a ship, or in a pioneering settlement. A fat lot of good they'll be as trappers."

"You can't leave them behind," said the Factor.

"I'll leave them or leave the lot," the Agent said. "The choice is yours—and I don't give a damn because you've paid for the ship."

The Factor reluctantly stepped forward and spoke to Duncan. "The Emigration Agent says the blind men cannot sail."

"And what do you say?" asked Duncan.

"I'm in his hands," said the Factor.

"A helpless bloody Factor you are," said Murchadh Ban, and there was a great roar of mirth. For the first time in their lives, the people of Ardvasar felt they were free from his domination, and he was being ordered around by a little runt of a Sassenach.

"I'm not leaving my brother here to die," said Duncan, and Norman stood beside him menacingly to give weight to his words.

The Factor looked at the Emigration Agent. The Emigration Agent shook his head. The men laughed again to see the Factor so easily put down.

Then their attention was diverted by a commotion in one of the small boats. Three of the women clambered ashore, taking their personal belongings with them. It was Murchadh Ban's brother's widow and the two young women who were widowed with her when a fishing boat was swamped.

They walked across to the Factor. "Will you leave three houses when you burn the rest?" they asked. The Factor nodded. "And you'll give us a little plot of land; we won't need much, our men have pensions." Again the Factor nodded.

The three women walked over to the blind soldiers, and

each took one by the arm. "We're staying with you," they said.

The men made no reply, but went with them up the hill, while the crowd on the beach watched them in silent amazement. When they had gone about twenty paces, Murchadh Ban's sister-in-law turned to them and said in Gaelic, "Our men may be blind, but their children will see."

"Come on, your lazy buggers," shouted the Emigration Agent. "Get moving or we'll miss the tide."

2

Lament for Ensay

It was winter and there was no moon, but the sky was clear and filled with frosty starlight. Although the tide was out, the great platter of firm sand known as the Cockle Ebb was still wet, so that the empty bay was like a broken mirror. There were flat stretches where the wet sand caught the glimmer of an incipient aurora, glowing with a general phosphorescence, but over much of the surface the tide was held in tiny pools between little 'worm casts' heaped up by the myriads of shellfish hidden below. The pools picked up the stars in little fragments of sky. Across one corner of the bay was the dark shadow of a single black cloud, low down on the northern horizon, from which the aurora was struggling free.

The crofters in Ardveenish and Ardnakille, lying opposite each other on the horns of the bay, thought nothing of crossing the Ebb when the tide was out, even in the dark. They could hear the Atlantic roar against the harbour bar away to the west, and they could tell by the sound the precise moment when the tide began to turn. They could gauge to a nicety whether they had time to cross before the sea came rushing back with all the weight of ocean behind it, in great, menacing, encircling sweeps. Even the children were familiar enough with the movements of the tide to make a game of it on frosty nights, skipping from star to star across the bay as city children do on mundane paving stones.

On this particular night, around 1820, it was late and the children were in bed, when two men crossed the bay at different times and in very different moods. Alastair Ban, the poet, who went first, strode, confident, across the stars. He felt as if he was riding a chariot through the sky or soaring like a bird higher than ever the eagle or the solan had aspired, and, as he went, he wrote a love song in his mind. Alastair Dubh, who, when he had a tiller in his hand, was perhaps the boldest man in Ensay, walked hesitantly as if he feared that at every step he might drop to eternity through a sky which had suddenly turned upside down. It was his own thoughts that disturbed him rather than the reflection on the sands with which he was familiar, and too much of a realist even to notice. At every step, the impulse to turn back was almost as great as the momentum of desire and wounded pride which drove him forward.

Although it was a good night for fishing and good nights are rare in the wild Hebridean winters, he had left his boat ashore, rejecting the advice of his father and the pleading of his mother, both of whom suspected what his errand was and feared that he might live to regret it.

"Will I help you bait the lines?" his mother had asked, as soon as she realised that the usual preparations for sea-going were not afoot.

"I won't need them tonight," he replied uneasily.

"It's a fine night," she suggested tentatively, but his father's brusque, "You'll never see a better," helped to stiffen his resolve.

"There's a storm brewing," he said with great firmness, but no conviction.

"There's a storm brewing, right enough," said his father, "but it's not the sort of storm you think it is."

Alastair Dubh strode out of the house.

"Do you really think he's going to Ardnakille?" asked his mother, as if the question might divert the danger, although she knew what the answer must be.

"A son of mine should have more sense than go sniffing around that silly bitch," he replied angrily. "If he had known her mother as long as I've known her, he would see what Peigi is and what she'll surely become."

"He's young yet," said his mother, now trying to shield him from his father's wrath.

"He's old enough to manage a boat. I don't see why he needs to be a fool with women."

His wife made no further comment, and, after a few minutes, he took down the family Bible and said, "Come, let us say the Books. If we can't pray with him, at least we can pray for him." He read a chapter, and prayed, and they sang a Gaelic psalm together, before she smoored the fire and they went to bed.

Alastair Dubh, as he made his way across the sands, could visualise them. He was, in fact, more aware of the scene at home, although he could not see it, than the stars around his feet. For one thing, it still had the impact of novelty. His father was a fairly recent convert, one of the few, so far, in Ensay, caught up in the religious movement which was reaching even the remoter islands, like a smouldering fire progressing almost unnoticed until it flared up in a highly emotional revival involving a whole community, only to burn itself out like a heath fire in the spring, leaving no obvious trace but a blackened landscape, although, beneath the ash, new life was stirring which would show itself later in fresh green shoots, fertilised by the debris of the burning. Alastair wished he had the courage to stand by his parents but he shrunk from exposing himself to the mockery of his contemporaries, and he was even more effectively deterred by the fear that, if he declared himself before he persuaded Peigi to marry him, he would lose her for good, whereas, if he won her first, he believed that he could carry her where, deep within him, he was already determined to go. He knew her reputation but refused to believe it. He struggled to ignore the hints and innuendoes of his companions, which was difficult enough when they arose spontaneously from idle chatter, and became increasingly burdensome when they realised the situation and began to invent adventures for her with Rabelaisian extravagance just for the pleasure of baiting him.

Paradoxically, it was a pleasure to bait him precisely because they shared his own ambivalence towards the strange elements from without which were gradually influencing their lives, and would eventually produce a new structure for a society which for several generations had been wallowing about in a void without landmarks or visible horizon. The more uncertain people are that their beliefs are well-founded, the more vociferously they cling to them, at least for the moment. Groups within a community which has lost its cohesion tend to polarise sharply but the groups themselves are unstable and, if one could watch them from a distance, and over a period of time, with the images speeded up, as when scientists photograph the burgeoning

34

of a flower and reproduce it on a time-scale the human eye can cope with, the movements within the community would have the appearance of an intricate dance with the partners continually changing until the old society is completely transformed and a new order has replaced it. For those involved in the whirl of the dance, however, all is confusion and confrontation.

Alastair Dubh's confrontation came as he left the beach and began to climb through the sand dunes towards Ardna-kille where, as the name indicates, there were the ruins of an ancient Celtic ecclesiastical centre, neglected and over-grown with noxious weeds, as was the teaching of the monks who built it, so that little now remained apart from the elements of superstition the monks themselves had in-herited from an earlier primitive culture, and which had shown greater powers of survival through the subsequent centuries of internecine strife, defeat and oppression, by alien conquerors and renegade native chiefs, which had subdued the spirit of the islanders and reduced their society to a state of resentful but spiritless anarchy, completely passive in the face of injustice because they were without leader or identifiable goal.

As Alastair Dubh rounded the corner of the church where the nettles were kept in check to some extent, at least, by the passage of many feet on the shortest path from the village to the beach, he saw a familiar figure coming towards him. Despite the darkness, he had no difficulty in identifying the swagger of Alastair Ban.

The two Alastairs, Fair and Dark, epitomised the main genetic strands in the community, Viking and Celt, but the passage of the centuries had so intermingled them that the landsmen and poet had the fair hair of the Norsemen, while the seamen, one of the greatest the island ever produced, was squat, broad-shouldered, and black, looking as if he had just emerged from a burrow in one of the prehistoric underground villages which are sometimes exposed by the shifting sands along the Atlantic coast of the Outer Hebrides, as at Skara Brae in Orkney.

Alastair Ban was one of Alastair Dubh's most persistent tormentors. He had the poet's facility for inventing amorous escapades in which he figured with Peigi, and the redder Alastair Dubh's cheeks became, the harder he plied the bellows of his wit, like a blacksmith softening the metal for the hammer strokes administered by the cruder blows of their less sensitive companions.

Alastair Ban was himself in love with Peigi in an intermittent sort of way. Her beauty stimulated him intellectually rather than physically. At times he sought and won her favours, but he had no illusions about her character, no wish to establish any exclusive rights with her, and certainly no intention of becoming permanently attached, and so limiting his poet's freedom to worship wherever he could find inspiration and companionship. He was her male counterpart, enjoying love without the encumbrance of rules, prohibitions, or regrets, but with sufficient seriousness to give a little edge of rival's malice to his baiting of Alastair Dubh.

On this occasion, however, he had been himself forestalled. As he approached her house, he saw another of Peigi's lovers creeping in. His own urgency had exhausted itself in the walk across the bay and, more particularly, in the love song he had composed, and he was amused by the stranger's obvious anxiety to slip in unnoticed rather than frustrated by his own ill-luck. He smiled to himself, and turned back towards his home in Ardveenish, composing another poem, a bawdy ballad for the boys about his own discomfiture, a grotesque parody of the imperishable love song he had created in his mind as he danced across the stars to his abortive tryst.

He had just completed the opening verse and was relishing it, as he fixed it in his memory, when a violent blow sent him reeling backward. Alastair Dubh, who had hidden in the shadows when he saw his namesake approaching, concluded that he had just come from Peigi's bedroom, and fell on him with all the fury of envious, frustrated, guilty, confused and tormenting desire.

It was a short fight but a savage one. Alastair Ban was taller than his adversary and almost as powerful. He quickly recovered and they closed with each other in fury. Fortunately they grappled closely. If they had exchanged blows in the mood they were in, one of them might have been killed, but their anger spent itself in a furious wrestling to and fro in the narrow path as they sought to wear each other down. Eventually they fell. Still locked together, they rolled among the nettles at their deepest until hands, arms and faces, even their ears and eyelids, were pock-marked with weals, and the itchy agony they suffered during the night became a proverb in Ensay—"Itching like the two Alastairs". The proverb is still used by children in another island who know what it means but not how it came by the meaning, nor the scene of the fight.

When eventually they parted among the nettles, they shot to their feet with the speed of springs released. Alastair

Dubh lunged at his opponent, who side-stepped smartly, avoiding the blow, but putting his foot unguardedly on one of the loose stones from the crumbling wall around the churchyard. He lost his balance and fell backward over the wall to the beach, ten feet below. Without stopping to see whether he was alive or dead, Alastair Dubh swung round and made for home filled, like an egg, with pride in his achievement.

He also experienced a curious but intense feeling of self-righteous exaltation because he, the unsullied, had thrashed a man who had been lying with a woman to whom he was neither married nor engaged, a self-righteousness reinforced, rather than diminished, by the knowledge, which he concealed from himself, that it was only his opponent's misdemeanour (which had not, in fact, occurred) which had saved himself from the identical sin.

Half-way across the sands he realised that the tide had turned and he must run to safety. At the same time, he remembered Alastair Ban and wondered whether he was lying senseless where the tide would get him. For a moment individual envy, masquerading as morality, whispered, 'Let the bastard drown', but then the reflex response inbred by the close-knit community supervened almost as if, in a flash, all the incidents in a youth of happy friendship had flooded into his mind, together with the realisation that their recent rivalry united rather than separated them, because it redefined more sharply than before, in terms of manhood, replacing those of childhood, their respective roles within the society to which they both belonged, and which was dependent for its survival on the willingness of each to help the other for the sake of all. Whatever the mechanism, or the ingredients, in the instantaneous process of thought, he turned again for Ardnakille, and ran until his strength was spent.

By the time he reached the sand dunes, the sea was clutching at his ankles and racing far beyond him towards the crofts. He clambered through the dyke with difficulty and down to the beach again at the point where Alastair Ban had disappeared. There was no trace of him, although he could see the mark at the top of the bank where he had displaced the stones and slithered over the edge. For a long time he searched up and down the beach, wading waist deep into the sea, in danger every moment of being carried away as the strength of the undertow grew and his own strength ebbed. Satisfied at last that Alastair Ban had escaped the incoming tide, he set off for home again, exhausted and anxious, but compelled to take a long way through the crofts and the machair, because the short cut across the sands was now open sea.

Alastair Ban, in the meantime, had made his way to one of the houses in the village where the local bone-setter bound up his broken arm. The job was done efficiently enough, considering that the bone-setter was quite without training or appliances, but the break was an awkward one, and, when the bone mended, his left hand was half-turned towards the front, as if he were seeking alms. Quite apart from the proverb their wild fight inspired, Alastair Ban earned from it the nickname of 'Beggar Ban', which followed him to the other island where the proverb still lives on. It was never used to his face, or by his friends, but only in reference to him by those who felt separated from him in a now deeply divided community. Although Gaelic was the language of Ensay in those days, and few islanders spoke any English at all, the foreign word was borrowed for the nickname, which somehow seemed appropriate because the whole incident had an alien, divisive aspect. No one reasoned through it; indeed, they were incapable, as we all are, of seeing ourselves in the perspective of a history which had not yet happened; nevertheless, with a sensitivity to mood which more formally educated generations have lost, they saw in the events of the week of which the fight was the dramatic beginning, a sudden change in the direction, or at least the climate, of their lives.

In the morning, the Ground Officer came to Ensay by boat for the immemorial and important ceremony of drawing lots for the machair strips for the ensuing spring. Every family in the two villages had a right to eight separate narrow strips of land for cultivation on the flattest part of the machair. In the spring, the strips were heavily fertilised with dung and seaweed, and the crops were planted as soon as the earth was warm enough. The children took turns all summer in keeping the cattle away from the growing crops because there was neither dyke nor fence but, in the autumn, after the harvest, the jealously guarded family strips were opened to the cattle and sheep of the two townships. The harvest was individual to the family group, the aftermath was shared by all.

Each year the strips were balloted for to make sure that every family, over a period of years at least, had a share of the good land and the bad. This tradition of social justice, complete equality of opportunity, was deeply rooted, and although it was obvious that some families fertilised their land and weeded it with more care than others, everyone

40

accepted the fact that these nourished acres went into the ballot with the rest, and the man who had laboured to raise the fertility of his little fragments of land might find himself struggling next year with a weed-infested legacy left him by a slovenly neighbour. It did not quite destroy the incentive to improve, but it certainly blunted the edge.

Although no one grumbled at his ill-luck or crowed openly if he drew a bargain, the fact that there were prizes and forfeits, at least in the short run, created an excitement below the calm, all the more keenly felt because it was suppressed. It showed itself in a disposition to chatter inconsequentially as if they were all mildly aroused by drink. Although they took no part in the draw, the women and many of the children, to say nothing of innumerable sheepdogs, attended the event which became in effect a huge outdoor ceilidh in which the residents of the two villages mixed more freely than on almost any other occasion in the year except a wedding or a funeral.

On the morning after the fight, however, things did not run their usual course and, although there was no immediate connection, people thereafter associated the two events, not only because of the juxtaposition in time and in the communal consciousness, but because of the sense that they were unrelated parts of a pattern not yet fully seen.

The Ground Officer was, surprisingly, accompanied by the Factor, a man of great power, greater in the crofters' eyes than the master who employed him, because he was the visible embodiment of authority while the landlord was remote and indefinite, the merest shadow of the chiefs of old though, like a shadow, black and disagreeable. The Chief might be the brain or even the arm behind their oppression,

41

but the Factor was the thong which seared their backs.

Instead of organising the cutting of stalks of grass of different lengths so that each crofter could draw his destiny for the coming season, the Ground Officer beckoned to the people to gather round him, and the Factor, standing on a hummock of sand to raise him above them, prepared to speak.

"Like Moses of old," he began, "I am going to lead you out of this captivity into the Promised Land."

The crofters looked at each other, bewildered. What captivity? They were poor and rack-rented and leaderless, but they were conscious of no captivity. They accepted their lot as they accepted the wind that blew and the rain that fell. Their neighbours on the islands round about were as poor as they, so they had no spur of envy or emulation. They had the tradition of a golden age remote and glittering but, however much one laments the loss of time past, one cannot aspire to recover it. Even a child can distinguish between reality and make-believe and, however real they thought the golden age had been, it now belonged to the realm of song and story which, like make-believe, was not quite part of life as it must be lived.

"This island is too small for you. Your numbers are growing. There are too many mouths to feed." The Factor droned on. Few of them followed in its entirety his indirect and highly allusive approach to the news that they were being turned out of their homes and land to begin life anew in Rona, an island which was alien, hostile, and repugnant to them, although they saw it every day rising out of the sea mist on the near horizon.

Movement of any sort was unwelcome. They were wedded

42

to the soil. To the particular soil they knew and cared for and had, in a sense, created. The static, egalitarian society in which no one could climb was attached to its meagre fields with the tenacity of the limpet, and almost without the limpet's power of voluntary release. When they learned that they were to be moved to Rona their vague apprehension became, for most of them, a panic fear.

As the Factor had said, there were now too many mouths for Ensay to feed. If he had suggested that some of them should emigrate to America or Australia, to leave more arable land for the rest, they would have seen sense in it and, although few of them would have been willing to go from choice, they might even have been ready to abide by the drawing of lots as they did in the allocation of the fields. But to move them all to Rona seemed an outrage and absurdity. Ensay was much the most fertile of the islands in the little archipelago. Rona was roughly the same size but, instead of level machair rimmed with gentle hills, it was a bleak, grey rock with no soil apart from little pockets of water-logged peat between outcrops of impervious gneiss which offered nourishment for no higher form of life than a scraggy lichen which spread across the weather-beaten surfaces between the peat hags like ringworm on an ageing head.

As soon as the significance of the Factor's message became clear, the whole community broke into little groups talking excitedly together, the men arguing and blaspheming, denouncing the proposal to each other because they dare not denounce it to the Factor; the women weeping, and the children chattering excitedly to see so much hysteria bubbling unexpectedly around them. The Factor rested his arms on his shepherd's crook, and his chin on his arms, and watched them with mild amusement.

"We'll let them simmer down for a little," he said to the Ground Officer. "They'll soon get used to the idea." Even he was surprised, however, when Alastair Dubh stepped forward to the hummock, pushed him aside, so that he could mount the little platform himself, and began to address his fellow islanders with impassioned eloquence.

"Insurrection!" said the Ground Officer to his superior. "I told you we would need the military to put this through." But Alastair Dubh's very first words revealed that his intention was very different from what they expected. He was not leading an insurrection but a revolution.

"The Factor is right," he said. "We'll be better on Rona than we are here. Provided he gives it to us for the same rent." As he mentioned rent, he looked at the Factor with a boldness and hostility that showed that he was not in any sense bowing to authority. "Will you?" he demanded. The Factor, taken off his guard, assented, a weakness for which he was later reprimanded by his chief.

Alastair's listeners were startled. "There's not enough on Rona to feed a rabbit," said Alastair Ban, quietly enough, because he did not want to give the impression that he was pursuing a vendetta because of the fight, which had been the principal topic of discussion until the Factor exploded his bomb.

"You can't grow potatoes on a lump of stone," agreed Padruig Dhomhnuill, a wizened old man who looked all of his eighty years, although he was still spry enough to potter round the family croft.

"There's not enough land to live on here, however good

44

it is," said Alastair Dubh.

"Maybe," said Alastair Ban, "but at least there's enough to dig a grave. What will we do with Padruig if we're sent to Rona?"

The little touch of humour took some of the desperation out of their mood and for a moment they all looked at Padruig and smiled.

"You'll have more than me to bury if we're sent to that barren rock," said Padruig. "No one has ever lived there. No one will ever live there." He turned full face to the Factor and spoke with a boldness that surprised them. "You might as well shoot us as send us to Rona. Perhaps," he added grimly, "you're grudging the powder and shot."

"Fools, fools, fools!" shouted Alastair Dubh. "No one expects you to live on rocks. But look at the ocean, stretching as far as the eye can see. Teeming with fish. Look at the boats that come from the South and from the East to make a fortune out of our sea. We sweat and scrape for a few potatoes and a little barley from this grudging earth, while they buy claret from the smugglers to quench their thirst. Rona has the one thing Ensay lacks—an anchorage for boats. Instead of fishing now and then, when the sea is calm, in a small boat that cannot venture further than the mouth of the bay, we can fish all the year round, with able sea boats, for herring, and mackerel and haddock and cod and ling and lythe. There are riches we never dreamed of lying out there, waiting to be lifted from the limitless ocean. A harvest all the year round without ploughing, or sowing, or weeding or stooking. A harvest that cannot be rotted by the rain. A harvest that's ready for gathering the moment your net goes into the sea."

"How many nets have you?" asked Alastair Ban.

It was a shrewd thrust, None of them had the capital to buy nets, let alone boats. The Factor saw his opportunity and retrieved his earlier mistake.

"I will provide the nets and the boats," he said. "You will be as well equipped as any fishermen in the world."

He was pleased with himself, because he could make up in interest what he had weakly given away in rent, and the interest would accrue to him, not to his master, the owner of the land.

"The island is already divided into crofts," he said. "I have been working while you have been lying in bed enjoying your winter sleep."

He grew expansive at the thought of personal gain. "I will give the best crofts to the men who take the first boats. Don't all rush together!"

Alastair Dubh raised his hand.

"That's one!" said the Factor. "Who's next?"

Without a word to the Factor or to each other, the men, as if acting on a command, turned about and walked away. The women followed, equally silent, and the children, who were reluctant to leave the scene of action, but were drawn by an irresistible, ebbing tide. Even the dogs caught the prevailing mood and followed their masters with their heads and tails subdued.

Alastair was left alone, facing the Factor. From a distance, his mother looked back, like Lot's wife, torn between her son and the unspoken condemnation of the whole community.

"Well," said the Factor, "what of it? You will go and they will be sent. I promised you the best croft. I'll do more than

46

that. I'll knock two crofts together and give you an estate."
He laughed a little ironically when he pictured the estate.
Rona was such a miserable place agriculturally that to
double a croft was to increase the burden rather than the
produce.

"I will draw lots with the rest," said Alastair, and turned
to follow them.

That night his father was surprised when Alastair joined
him at family worship. It may have been merely a craving
to identify with some group, even the small circle of his own
family, because of his apparent rejection by the larger community. It may have been frustrated love, or revulsion from
the knowledge that he had been forestalled with Peigi. It
may have been ambition: the feeling that, even if he had
been rejected, he had discovered the power of speaking in
public which could be exercised most successfully through
the revivalist movement. Or it may have been that he sensed
that the old society, already crumbling, would be irretrievably broken by the forced move to Rona, and that only an
intense religious experience could fuse them together again
although, for the moment at least, it was an experience the
great majority disdained. Most probably, all these elements
were present in some degree, as the rain and the sun, the
minerals hidden in the soil, and even the organic debris left
by the decay of earlier vegetation all nourish the new growth.
The essential seed was planted by the Factor, whose image
of Moses leading the children of Israel to the promised land
gave Alastair a clear vocation: in the new situation they
were being driven into, his skill as a seaman and his power
as a preacher would make him inevitably leader.

When he went to bed that night, he prayed silently to

himself, as if fanning the dull embers of his father's words into a blaze of passionate pleading with the Almighty to send him as a pillar of fire before them to lead his people into their new life on Rona.

And, although they had spurned him at the meeting with the Factor, more and more of the islanders came round to join their worship at nights, and, as Alastair Dubh himself took over from his father as leader in prayer, the numbers increased more rapidly, and the young folk joined their elders round the family fire. After the service, they went out into the darkness, not with the warm-milk feeling of communal friendship, nor the terror of ghosts and witches, which they took in different moods from the ceilidhs of old, but with a great sense of being uplifted so that they triumphed over the drudgery of their daily lives. One could identify those who were converted by a confidence, almost a jauntiness, in their step, as they walked about the crofts to do their common chores. Among the converts was Peigi, who dragged her mother reluctantly along.

Peigi had been elated when she heard of the fight between the two Alastairs. Though gossip had not deterred her in the past from going her own way, it had sometimes touched her pride, but now she could walk forth boldly as the uncrowned queen of Ensay, the beauty for whom strong men fought. Or so it seemed in the rosy flush of morning, when the story first began to circulate, but, instead of following up his victory by coming to plead for her love, Alastair Dubh had become a morbid preacher, denouncing all sin in phrases of devouring eloquence, and above all else, the sin from which only the encounter with his rival had saved himself. Moreover, her other admirers, knowing what had happened to Alastair Ban, and not being convinced that Alastair Dubh's conversion was complete or permanent, kept their distance from the flame round which they had danced so merrily, in case he dealt as directly with them.

When she watched the encounter with the Factor, she was the only one in Ensay who sided wholeheartedly with Alastair Dubh. She admired him, not because she agreed with what he had to say—she did not even try to understand it—but because she felt the courage and the eloquence were in a sense her own. She expected to see him at her door at nightfall to make his submission and claim his prize.

"If he sails his boat like that, it won't be long till he drowns," said her mother, as they walked home together towards their home which stood a little apart from the others in the village. "That man could be a king!" replied Peigi. "And he's right! He's right! We would be better far in Rona than in this dreary place."

Her mother was astonished at Peigi's stupidity. "Here at least you have straw for your bed," she replied. "How would you fancy sleeping on a bag of stones?"

In choosing that particular illustration of the poverty of Rona, the old woman was not getting at her daughter's way of life. It had been her own, and she saw no harm in it. She had lived almost with the simplicity of the animals and with their innocence. She accepted each passing moment as it came, and she still enjoyed the company of the young men who came around the house because of her daughter's beauty, of which she was even vainer than Peigi herself. The only point on which they differed was Alastair Dubh.

Previously, Peigi had longed for him and hated him. He seemed cold, aloof, and supercilious. When his name was

49

mentioned she would dismiss him contemptuously as 'that proud skate', but there was an overtone, or perhaps an undertone, in her voice which was more eloquent than the words she used. When she heard of the fight she was triumphant because she knew at last that he was not insensitive to her power. "He may think I'm there for the asking," she said with a toss of her head. "He'll find out different."

Her mother, free from passion, and seeing Alastair with the eye of experience, and with knowledge of his parents and grandparents, thought him a dangerous man who should be kept at a distance. "He's not for you," had been her invariable comment when they discussed him, and her view of him was reinforced when she learned that he had become a preacher.

With Peigi it was different. Her triumph turned to despair. At the same moment almost, she had discovered that Alastair Dubh was vulnerable—and unattainable. For the first time in her life she was distressed by love, she who had enjoyed so much the distress she caused in others. She was drawn to Alastair simultaneously by aroused desire and the need to assert herself. She wished with equal passion to submit to him and to dominate him, to possess and be possessed. Like a complex movement in music which unites all the instruments of the orchestra in a multitudinous harmony, each making its own distinctive sound in its own characteristic way, but all combining towards a single outcome, every element in her, from the primitive instinct she shared with the animals and which subordinates the individual for the purposes of the species, to the exclusive personal pride which, according to Milton, alone separates us from the angels, directed her thoughts towards the house where her lover slept and ate and preached and went out and in to pursue his calling as a fisherman. Nothing would have pleased her better than to have the right, which married women had in respect of their husbands, to carry him on her back through the surf to his boat so that he could begin his journey to the fishing grounds dry, while she returned to strip and change and hang her sodden underwear around the peat fire while she awaited his return.

She pleaded with her mother for days, using all sorts of pretexts by which the old woman was not deceived, before she succeeded in persuading her to go with her to a service in Alastair Dubh's, not as chaperon—the idea was as foreign to her as the word—but as cover, alike for the helpless nakedness with which she threw herself at his feet, and her arrogant, calculating, overweening ambition to humble him in the presence of his fellow worshippers.

On her first visit, Peigi walked boldly in and sat herself in a conspicuous place from which she could match the power of her eyes against the eloquence of the preacher's tongue. The congregation sighed at her shamelessness but delighted in her presence, because they sensed that they were watching a duel between well-matched adversaries. They prayed that they would see her put down and humbled by the power of God, but secretly they hoped that the drama might be long drawn out. None of them were conscious of the element of human jealousy—the men of Alastair and the women of Peigi—which reinforced their righteousness and sweetened their joy.

They were even less aware, because it was concealed, of the torment Alastair suffered. Every look, every quiver of her voice as she sang; her sly, upturned glance as she pretended to pray, her bold assault when he was preaching and she caught his eye directly, was like a dart, unnoticed at the moment of impact, which does its deadly work long after the encounter, as the poison from its tip spreads through the body in hours of solitude and darkness and seeming ease.

The congregation was astonished by his impassivity. He was not, apparently, embarrassed or distracted by Peigi's bold assault, in fact he prayed for her openly, almost by name, seeking the redemption of a fallen sister. Publicly his love for her was dead. Only pity remained. But after the nightly service it was different, and through the hours when he should have been asleep, he writhed and shivered and fought in his imagination with Satan, in the form of a beautiful woman, with a violence that tore him apart.

The sleeplessness he endured did not undermine Alastair's resolution either as a preacher or a leader; it gave added force to his eloquence and organising power as each morning he bounded back into the feverish action preparing for Rona, in which he hid from his torment.

As a result of Alastair Dubh's activities, the community was divided into two factions of almost equal size numerically by the time the Factor took the next move towards their eviction. One faction was growing in numbers, confident in their purpose, but submissive, for reasons of their own, to the Factor's will. The other was weak and dispirited, without an identifiable leader or a clear purpose although, to the end, they maintained a half-hearted show of resistance to the tyranny which all alike resented, even those who bowed beneath the yoke.

The Factor misread the situation. He assumed that Alastair Dubh had remained the solitary acquiescent. Indeed, he reckoned that the pressure of opinion within the community would force him back into line with the others. He had experienced recalcitrance among the crofters in other townships where, for his own reasons, or his master's he had taken similar action, and he was determined to run no risks with his plan to clear Ensay for sheep. The prize was too enticing: an increased rent for Ensay from a prosperous farmer, an equal rent for Rona which hitherto had paid no tribute at all, and the prospect of usury, as the crofters struggled to develop the fishings, and he squeezed them to the limit for their boats and gear.

So it was that a Messenger at Arms from the Court in Edinburgh arrived at Ensay to serve summonses of removal against the crofters. The Messenger had been warned to expect resistance, and when a few callow youths crowded about him shouting spiritless words of defiance in a language he did not understand, he acted as if he were faced with a major riot.

He mounted a hummock, as the Factor had done, and addressed the youths. He explained his office, and his function, and the authority behind him. He then solemnly exhibited his blazon and his wand of peace, and with a great dramatic show he broke the wand, and warned them of the consequences of resistance in any form. The youths were fascinated by the pantomime, as it was to them, for the Messenger's language was quite as incomprehensible to them as theirs had been to him, and even those of them who had some smattering of English could make nothing of the high-flown legal terms in which the warning was couched. Someone threw a clod which struck the Messenger's blazon and they all scattered in different directions laughing at the strange behaviour of the visitor and their own daring.

Apart from that little incident, the Messenger was un-molested as he moved from house to house delivering the summonses but, when he returned to the mainland, he reported in great detail how by his timely action he had quelled a dangerous disturbance. Impressed by the gravity of the situation, the authorities arranged that the eviction, when it actually took place, would be supervised by the police, supported by marines and bluejackets.

Alastair Ban and Alastair Dubh both watched the encoun-ter between the youths and the Messenger at Arms from a distance, but with very different emotions. To Alastair Dubh the summonses were irrelevant. He was determined to go, whether forced from the island or not. He even derived a cynical pleasure from the thought that the Factor was being used as a pawn by the Almighty, so that his very greed would save them from the growing hunger on Ensay, where year by year the increase in population outstripped the produce of the little crofts. To Alastair Ban the Messenger came directly from the Prince of Darkness, decreeing the destruction of their homes, their language, their songs, and their coherence as a people. He saw the revival as a form of madness, destroying all that was pleasurable in lives which were otherwise nothing but unremitting toil, and Alastair Dubh as a Judas conspiring with Satan from within the very heart of the community.

That night, for the very first time since the fight, Alastair Ban visited Peigi. He felt an urgent desire to let her hear the love song he had composed as he walked across the Ebb among the stars. Like everyone else in Ensay, he was aware of the tension between her and Alastair Dubh, although none of them knew precisely how things stood nor could foresee, with any certainty, the final outcome. He was not so much concerned to win Peigi with his song as to assert the power of music, poetry and human love in the face of the preacher who sought to subordinate them to the iron rule and bureaucratic discipline of a kirk session.

In the past, there would have been a crowd of young men round the peat fire by the time Alastair Ban arrived at Peigi's home. Apart from the attraction of Peigi herself, it was a free and easy home, where song and story and local gossip were uninhibited, and many young men came to ceilidh there who would never have ventured to visit Peigi on her own. Her favours were reserved for the few, and even they could not count on them: Peigi derived more pleasure from tantalising men than from submitting to them.

Alastair Ban, however, found Peigi's mother entirely alone. Since mother and daughter had begun to attend the services at Alastair Dubh's, the evening ceilidhs had come to an end, and it was now a dismal house without the merrymaking of the old regime or the confident self-righteousness of the new.

"It's a poor fireside this, for a man to warm his hands at," was the mother's greeting to Alastair Ban. She was glad to see him because she was still being dragged reluctantly by her daughter to services she would herself have avoided. She saw Alastair Ban as her last hope to check the flowing tide of the revival before they were all submerged.

"It's just like the ocean," she said to him, pointing to the open sands which he had just crossed. "You see it darting here and there, and before you know what's happening, it's

55

snapping at your ankles like an angry dog and you're cut off from the land.

"What can live in the sea, anyway?" she asked rhetorically. "Nothing but cold, slimy fish."

Alastair Ban laughed. "I wouldn't call Alastair Dubh a cold fish," he said. "When he's preaching there's nothing hotter this side of hell."

"He doesn't burn with fire," said the old woman with unexpected venom. "He burns with ice. Fire melts, but that man gets harder day by day."

She broke off sharply when Peigi came in. It was clear that mother and daughter saw things differently.

Peigi welcomed Alastair Ban and spoke to him freely like her old self until he began quietly humming the tune to which he had set his love song.

"What's that?" she asked sharply.

"A little song I wrote for you," he replied. "You would have heard it long ago but I had a little accident." He raised his injured arm. It was his intention to make light of his encounter with Alastair Dubh, but still to remind her that he was the one who had suffered on her account. His joke had quite the wrong effect, and Peigi's reply stunned him.

"You will not sing ungodly songs in this house," she flared. "You will not mock the man on whom my salvation depends. You dragged me down with the others and now you hate, and bait, and harass the only man who can lift me up again." She burst into tears and fled from the room.

"He's put the evil eye on her," said her mother to comfort the astonished visitor.

Without replying Alastair Ban rose and went out, ironically humming to himself the song to his beloved which now she would never hear. But, though he made a pretence of singing, his mind was anxious with dark and troubled thoughts. As he passed through the old churchyard, towards the path across the sands, he heard a rustling as if the ghosts were stirring from the tombs around him. The ghosts of all the men and women who had lived and loved and fought and sang in Ensay back through the ages to the time when hooded monks worshipped in the ruined church itself, and the men going into battle wore coats of mail like the warrior whose effigy could still be faintly seen on a large stone in one of the walls. He knew the sound was probably a sheep pushing through the nettles to a patch of grass, but he could not be sure, and in his despondent mood he did not want the security of commonplace facts. He quickened his step as he felt a chill which was not, he thought, the chill of evening but something deeply sinister moving near him. He hurried on until he reached the sands where the sound of the sea warned him that the time for crossing was short. Pursued, as he felt himself to be, by an evil spirit, he decided it was safer not to risk the beach, and he turned inland towards the machair and the low hills beyond.

The tension eased as he got among the cultivated strips, where the work of human hands was evident all about him, and the men and women who tilled the strips seemed physically present. When he came to the open machair, he visualised it as it would be in high summer when the trefoil patterned it with sheets of gold as far as the eye could reach. As he mounted the hillocks at the Ardveenish end and looked back over the machair, and the black plots of cultivated ground, and the thatched houses crouching like sleeping animals in every sheltered hollow, his heart filled with the memory of all the joy of all the generations which had gone before him. He was exalted as he had never been before with the love of place and people and the sense of a long continuity of human fellowship, of which he himself was part. Then he felt as if the ground were moving beneath his feet and all the familiar objects began to change before his eyes and take new shapes, grey, bleak, sterile and repugnant. His beloved Ensay had changed as he watched into the hated, uninhabited wilderness of Rona. He took it as a sign that it was no longer a matter of choice whether or not they would go to Rona, or even whether they would be driven there by the Factor. He saw Rona approaching inevitably, irresistibly, like doom.

It was there, in the chill of the night, sitting alone on the hillside until dawn was breaking, that Alastair Ban composed one of the great laments of the Gael. It far transcends in scope and feeling the songs composed by emigrants banished in leaky plague-ridden ships to Cape Breton Island or Hudson Bay, where they had to hew homes and fields out of the virgin forest in a climate harsher than they had ever known. Alastair Ban had not yet left his native island and, at the worst, he was moving only a few miles away to another island he had always known, and from which, on a clear day, the low line of his beloved Ensay would always be visible. Perhaps it was the thought that Ensay would be so close though unattainable that gave wings to his verse, but in the darkness he composed a song in which the loss of Ensay represents the loss of everything the Gaels had cherished from the dawn of history to the point which Alastair Ban believed they had reached—the final dispersal of the race. And with the words the music came, a mint-new

58

tune which sparkled like the starlight or the machair flowers, as he sang the praises of Ensay, but shaded imperceptibly into a desolate keening as he described their departure from laughter and sunshine for the bleak, wind-swept rock on which he believed they were to perish.

The song went round the villages of Ensay like the fiery cross, leaping from lip to lip, and from house to house. Those who, like Alastair Ban himself, opposed the move to Rona and hated the revival, regarded it almost as a hymn of battle but, strangely, it was taken up by their opponents as well. It spoke for all of them in the deep places of the heart and, when eventually they sailed for Rona, the whole population, whether in a little boat, almost capsizing with the burden of people, livestock, ploughs and bedding, or still standing on the beach amid their miserable possessions awaiting their turn to sail, sung it together with an anguish that soared into the vault, and still echoes faintly round the homes in Rona today. The policemen with their batons, the marines and bluejackets with their muskets and bayonets, who were sent by a remote and bemused authority to prevent a riot, stood to attention in the soft Hebridean rain, watching the orderly, peaceful embarkation and listening without comprehension to the swelling song which echoed back and forth between the fleet of little vessels and the shore, until the first wave of migrants had passed beyond earshot and the others huddled silent in the rain to await the return of the boats.

In the first few months on Rona the words of Alastair Ban's lament were seared into their souls. In the space of weeks every family had to build a home and create a croft from the wilderness.

For the house, it was necessary to gather thousands of boulders and carry them in creels to the chosen site. Then, scratch among the scraggy patches of moorland between the rocks to get turf for the roof. There was not even straw or rushes for thatching. The building of a house in normal times was nothing, for the whole community joined together to complete the task. But in Rona there was no help to be had from neighbours because everyone simultaneously was homeless.

Surveying the sheet of gneiss, smoothed aeons before by the moving ice, Padruig Dhomhnuill spat explosively. "These bloody rocks are too mean even to have boulders," he said. "They're worse than Barabel's cow." The reference to the old maid's cow, which had been cherished until it died of old age although it had never dropped a calf, set them all laughing for a moment amid their misery but the comment was accurate enough because, except at the foot of the cliffs where the sea had done its work, creating almost inaccessible beaches, the rocks refused to yield up manageable stones in any quantity for the builders.

While most of the weary Ensay exiles wandered here and there across the barren landscape, picking up the odd piece of rock which did exist, Alastair Dubh got out his boat and sailed to a boulder beach. He was not much quicker in gathering his quota, nor was the task of loading and unloading and hauling the stones up the cliff-face path any easier than the task the others grappled with, but at least he was able to organise his work in an orderly way and avoid the frustration of vain searching. Some of the others eventually followed his example, grudgingly, it must be said, for they all felt that he had been mistaken in his judgement about Rona, and indeed some of them began to blame him personally for the Factor's ukase.

The making of the crofts was more laborious even than the building of the homes. It was not a case of breaking virgin soil resistant to the plough. There was no soil of any sort to take a plough, and the primitive implements they had transported with so much difficulty from Ensay had to be abandoned for the still more primitive cas chrom. And, before they could use the cas chrom, they had to assemble sufficient soil in one spot for the blade to bite on. Like ants, they moved in unbroken lines across the island, coming and going with creels of soil scraped here and there between the rocks, using even the debris of peat dust left in the little hollows from which they had taken the turf for the house roof. Again, it was Padruig who lightened the gloom with a shaft of wintry mirth. Gnarled and twisted and tough like an old thorn cromag—although the simile would not have occurred to them because Ensay and Rona were equally devoid of trees—he hirpled out one day holding aloft a little horn egg-spoon which was one of his few possessions. Everyone he met asked him where he was going with the spoon. "To dig the croft," he replied, and for a whole morning he could be seen vainly trying to fill a creel with tiny spoonfuls of peat dross, which spilt through the gaps in the basket-work as quickly as he poured them in.

When soil had been gathered, they had to get seaweed to fertilise it. On the flat beaches of Ensay the winter storms piled the tangle high, straight brown branches, as thick as a man's wrist, which smelt of fertility as they carried them off half rotted in the spring to add to the goodness of the manure heap, protected all winter from the leeching rain in the butt end of their homes, and which, from time to time, was still further enriched by the old straw from the roof, solid and black with the rich, nourishing soot of the peat-smoke. Every ounce of vegetable or mineral matter which had any manurial value was hoarded on Ensay and returned to the soil which sustained their lives. There was no waste, or prodigality, no short-term views—everything was geared to the survival of the community, except the size of the population which, as the Factor had seen, was rapidly out-stripping their resources, enabling him to cloak with spurious logic a decision dictated by greed.

Rona, with no beaches, had no tangle and, as the houses, such as they were, had newly been built, there was no straw or soot or manure or even ash. As Padruig put it crudely but succinctly, "On this bloody rock there isn't even shit."

Again, it was Alastair Dubh who was the innovator, the pioneer in a community which had known no spontaneous change for generations and perhaps centuries. He got out his boat and sailed at low tide to the reefs around the island, hacking off bladder-weed with a rusty sickle, and towing it back behind the boat in a huge raft loosely held with heather rope. It was a task which required the patience of Job and the strength of Hercules, but gradually he built a pyramid of seaweed on the beach, which the other members of the family then carried laboriously in creels to the croft, high above them on the hillside.

It did not escape notice that Peigi and her mother drew from the same pyramid. That, in itself, might have had no significance, because the spirit of neighbourliness was still strong, and the Factor by chance, or perhaps from spite, had allocated them adjacent crofts. What was remarked by

62

the islanders, sensitive to every little nuance in each other's behaviour, was the suppressed hostility between the two family groups, when Alastair Dubh was not around himself, and which bubbled to the surface in little putterings and squirts of steam like the volcanic springs which flare up from time to time, revealing the tumult of heat which is roaring far below.

Some of the other families followed Alastair Dubh's lead and went in search of seaweed with their boats, but few of them were so energetic or successful and, as he moved first, he had cleared the more accessible reefs before others got to them, which occasioned great bitterness because it was the first overt sign that, in their new environment, the old rules of equal sharing and equal misery were breaking down.

Another indication that they were in a new social environment as well as a new physical environment was given by a succession of squabbles, once or twice leading to threats or even blows, as to the areas of moor in which different families were entitled to gather heather, turf or soil. There was no rotational run-rig on Rona. One of the great advances made, in the Factor's view, was that each family had a self-contained holding so that the energetic could prosper, and so produce higher rents for the estate. But a great part of the high ground in the centre of the island was necessarily left in common. It was fit for summer grazing only, and hardly even for that. There were no rules, customs or precedents to regulate rights on the common land and, in the absence of the Ground Officer, who, when he was around, administered 'justice' with a firmness which was equalled only by its partiality and eccentricity, it fell to the older men in the community to smooth over the quarrels as they arose. This they did with fair success, and it was noticeable that Alastair Dubh was given no part in this process. Those who were listened to with most respect were those who had been opposed to the move from Ensay and had not yet succumbed to the religious revival. One could also detect a tendency for the two factions to support their own adherents in the quarrels, although they had nothing to do with religious points of principle, and a cynic might even have argued that the revivalists were just as ready to be grasping and illogical as those they denounced as unredeemed. Indeed, the revivalists were less constrained by old social usages than the others, because they belonged to a community 'not of this world'.

When Alastair boldly took his boat back to Ensay and loaded it with manure from the abandoned family homestead, the emotions of the broken community were very confused. Everyone, even those who hated him most, applauded his defiance of authority, and some were envious that they had not thought of it themselves, thus leaving the glory to the 'traitor' who had led them from their ancient paradise. However, when retribution overtook him, some, even of his own supporters, were glad to see him humbled.

He had got only one boat-load safely back to Rona when the new tenant of Ensay invoked the Factor's power. Alastair was arrested and taken to Inverness where he was locked in the cells for several days before appearing in front of the sheriff, charged with stealing the manure of his own cows from his own byre because it was now the property of the tenant who was paying rent for Ensay. He was fined five shillings, and was not released from custody until the fine had been paid by a merchant in the town whose family had belonged originally to Ensay and who still regarded Alastair Dubh as a distant cousin.

When Alastair returned to Rona, he was greeted by Padruig Dhomhnuill with the salutation, "Well, Alastair, you have come back to the promised land, where we all have two crofts: one in front of the house and another on the roof, and the one on the roof is the bigger of the two."

It was an exaggeration to say that a turf roof was bigger than even the smallest of the crofts, but it was not so far-fetched if one looked at the individual patches of which the crofts were composed, some of them, as Padruig had remarked on another occasion, "no bigger than a coffin and a damn sight draughtier."

Oddly enough, although Alaistair Dubh's judgement seemed totally discredited, the harder the crofters had to labour to survive through that first desperate season in their new home, and the more despondent they became, the more of them flocked to hear him preach. It was almost as if they were fleeing from the hardships of real life to take sanctuary in the spiritual kingdom which Alastair offered them.

The first stage in the occupation of Rona was the erection of rough shelters of tarpaulin and bags, like tinkers' tents, until their turf-thatched homes were ready. But the houses did not come next. Before the first house was started, under Alastair's impassioned leadership, they built a little thatched hut no bigger than a kitchen in which to hold their nightly worship. Not all of them assisted with the building but, as the days passed, more and more joined in, a little sheepishly at first, and then boldly, bringing others and, once it was in

C   65

use, some even of those who idly watched and sneered, attended the services.

The meeting-place completed, Alastair Dubh began to build his father's house. At the same time it was seen that he was applying almost equal energy to the building of another house, close by, on the croft assigned to Peigi and her mother.

The juxtaposition of the crofts made frequent contact inevitable, and in his exalted mood Alastair could not help seeing it as a sign from on high, except of course in his not infrequent moments of doubt, when he suspected that it might be the work of the Devil.

Before they left Ensay, Peigi had come in tears to the service and confessed her unrighteousness with a wealth of detail which made the meeting more entertaining than the ceilidh had ever been, although one would not have gathered that from the hushed voices and the sighs with which the congregation cloaked their enjoyment of Peigi's revelations, as they analysed and dissected them in the ensuing weeks. Apart from what she had to say, her passionate self-abasement was an exciting performance in itself, and many of them, doubting her sincerity, regarded it as no more than that. Alastair himself gave no sign that he saw her as in any way different from the others who had made similar confessions of other sins. He certainly gave no indication that Peigi's confession affected him personally, except in so far as he was pleased to welcome another convert to the cause. His secret torment, however, continued. Indeed it became more intense. He was torn between the triumphant knowledge that she was his for the asking and a reluctance to forgive, or forget, her past behaviour, which was strangely at variance with the message he preached. Envy of his less inhibited rivals had stoked the fire of passion when they had access to her but, now that she had repudiated them, she seemed tarnished in his sight in a way she had not previously been.

It was the practical business of giving aid to a helpless woman which resolved his dilemma. He could not avoid her or ignore her. He had to act. And, in doing so, he provided rare sport for those of the other faction who watched and sneered as he became daily more deeply entangled.

"In my Father's house are many mansions," said Padruig Dhomhnuill, picking up a phrase of which Alastair, in his preaching, made frequent use, and indicating with a nod the two houses rising side by side on the high ground much closer together than the boundaries of the crofts or the lie of the land necessarily demanded.

"She'll lead him a dance yet," said Alastair Ban, speaking with some knowledge of the 'she', and perhaps with a twinge of envy.

"God, yes!" said Padruig. "There's been nothing like it since the rabbit married the stoat."

"Yes," said Alastair Ban, adding with the poet's insight, "only time will tell which is the rabbit and which is the stoat."

"If you don't like my way of putting it, take Alastair's own," said Padruig. "He's never tired of telling us that the day will come when the lion lies down with the lamb."

"He'll lie with her, all right," said Alastair Ban. "The question is, will he be the only one?"

"It's a question which has occurred to him as well as to you," said Padruig. "Look at these two doors. A flea can't get in or out of Peigi's without him seeing it. By God, he won't get much sleep, night after night, with his eye to the spy-hole."

But much to the surprise of all, and the dismay of some, he married Peigi, and she became a model wife. She had undergone a genuine change, religious, physiological or emotional, or perhaps all three interacting together. She retained her hospitable nature, and so gave great strength to her much more reserved husband. Their home was as freely open to all-comers as the ceilidh house had been when Peigi presided there, so that there were always new visitors present in the process of becoming converts, but no one ever had occasion to point a finger at her, and Alastair Dubh himself eventually outgrew the anxiety and suspicion which was still lurking in his mind even when he stood beside her and a well-known revivalist preacher, who had come specially from the mainland for the occasion, pronounced them man and wife.

The success of his marriage strengthened Alastair Dubh by giving him peace of mind, but it did not add greatly to his stature in the community, because it was a negative sort of achievement, which only the slow-moving years confirmed, so that people took it for granted and forgot their own misgivings without ever realising that their judgement had been wrong and Alastair's vindicated.

It was different in the years of the famine, when it was apparent to all that they lived better in Rona on a monotonous diet of fish, than those in the more fertile islands round about, where the crops had failed and people scrabbled in the sand for razorfish, or on the rocks for limpets, or were even forced to gnaw the rods of tangle by

68

the hunger which pursued them day and night.

"If we were still on Ensay, we would be bleeding the cows just now," said old Padruig Dhomhnuill, shortly before he died. It was a bitter day in spring, when the stocks of food were always at their lowest, and sometimes, to make an appetising dish, they had actually bled the cows to make black puddings, thus rendering the last of the oatmeal a little more palatable.

Then he corrected himself. "If we were in Ensay now, we wouldn't have cows to bleed, or oatmeal to make puddings."

The old sparkle was gone. Nothing remained but the stark acceptance of a truth he had resisted. Alastair Dubh had been right: it was the move from Ensay that saved them.

Alastair was now free from the constraints of a community regulated by custom, wholly dependent on the harvest weather and, above all, submissive to a doctrine of rigid egalitarianism which left them lethargic when faced with the need for change, and envious of more enterprising neighbours when change was forced upon them, but which, in normal times, was like a warm blanket cast around them, keeping them huddled and united in the face of adversity. With the great majority of the islanders solidly behind him, he felt strong enough for other innovations.

"We must open a school," he said, and no one demurred, even when he approached the Factor for his help and guidance. The Factor took the matter to the proprietor, who offered an annual contribution to the Edinburgh Gaelic Schools Society if they would station a teacher on Rona for a period of years. Both the Factor and the people of Rona made much of the proprietor's generosity although, if the truth were told, he believed, according to his political principles, that in time a rising standard of education would be reflected in rising rents, while the Factor, for his part, ensured that the rents rose irrespective of the standard of education or even the ability to pay.

The school met in the original meeting-house, now replaced by a larger and more durable building. Seated on planks of driftwood, gathered from the shore, or even on little heaps of peat, the pupils sat in darkness lightened only by the gentle glow from the fire in the middle of the floor, the effect of which was largely offset by the lazy, blue, aromatic smoke which issued from the same source and filled the room. There was no blackboard or books. The alphabet was written in large characters on sheets of paper held up before them while the pupils repeated the unfamiliar names for the symbols which could make the printed Bible speak to them. At times, the teacher used his walking stick to write a word on the earthen floor, but that was only effective on dry days when the door stood open and a shaft of light illuminated a patch of floor towards the middle of the room where all could see it.

The pupils themselves were of all ages and both sexes, although the women and girls were few. The children had to be coaxed, cajoled and sometimes even beaten to make them attend, but their elders went avidly and humbly, seeking a key to the knowledge of God which, they believed, alone could make them free.

The ability to read and write unlocked other doors as well, new vistas of knowledge none of them had dreamed of, and opportunities of worldly advancement at war with their primary motive which quite simply and purely was to

70

attain a surer knowledge of the world to come.

Alastair Dubh was delighted with the success of the school in which he was himself one of the most diligent pupils, often giving up a good fishing day to attend, as he had done once before for very different reasons but with far-reaching consequences, of which the school was one. But it was some time before he learned of something which delighted him even more than the sight of a full classroom.

His old rival, Alastair Ban, who had kept aloof when all the others had succumbed to the new discipline, had secretly made a bargain with one of his neighbour's children. The lad, who was one of the brightest in the little school, was offered the reward of a lamb—no mean gift—if, after every lesson, he would go to Alastair Ban and teach him all that he had learned.

Alastair Ban was almost the only member of the community who was not now a regular churchgoer. Secular songs were sung only surreptitiously, if sung is the word, for they were rather rolled over silently in the mind, by some of the older folk, and Alastair, who had been the centre and life of the community for so many years, was an outcast, almost a hermit, alone and neglected on the periphery.

Alastair Dubh was wrong in taking the news about Alastair Ban as a triumph for himself, at that stage anyway. The poet of their old communal life was more sensitive than others to the change in the general atmosphere, but he still regarded it as a long hard winter of the spirit which would eventually pass. His one aim was to ensure that the old things survived against the spring which he foresaw. With a sharper vision than the others, he realised that the ability to read and write could be put to more uses than one, although he had no inkling of the wider possibilities and, if he had, would have been less interested in them than Alastair Dubh himself. Alastair Ban was not concerned with the life to come, but equally he was not concerned with the secular future; his one aim was to preserve the past and, if possible, to restore it: to reoccupy the crumbling ruins in Ensay now disappearing beneath drifting sand, and even to repeople them with the men and women of his own childhood or a new generation fashioned precisely like them.

He learned to read only because he wished to write. Reading by itself could lead only to a study of the Bible which he regarded superstitiously with both veneration and hostility. His purpose was to set down for future generations as much as he could remember of the traditions of his race and, night after night, alone in his hut, apart from his youthful teacher, he laboured with the alphabet, writing on a board across his knees, in a jotter acquired with great difficulty and great expense, on a journey he undertook to the mainland for that specific purpose.

In the end, however, the isolation was too much for him. He craved company, and when he sought it, he inevitably came under the prevailing influence in the community. He began to realise that the new church bound them just as securely together as the old semi-pagan social customs, with their faint echoes of the teaching of the Celtic church, and embodied a form of egalitarianism which appealed to him all the more because it was rooted—as egalitarian communities and groups so often are—in an exclusive elitism, open and free to all—provided they submit to its demands. The liberating and disruptive forces being released by the school

72

had not yet manifested themselves, and would do so slowly, over several generations and so, in ignorance of the future, he was content to seek acceptance from the community in which he lived on the terms on which it would receive him.

Alastair Ban became a convert in spite of his determination to resist, and instead of the ancient lore of his people, he wrote in his jotter spiritual songs, reflecting the mood of the community of which he was, by instinct, the mirror.

He wrote them partly to exercise the new facility he had acquired with so much effort, but also to quiet his conscience. He wished to leave behind him, as a permanent memorial, godly songs which would obliterate the memory of the vain trifles which had occupied his youth and which fortunately, as he saw it, had no material existence because they had never been committed to paper.

In this intention he was frustrated, although he never knew it. His new songs did not have the quality to give them independent life, although they did have a short vogue on Rona and, so far as the written version was concerned, it was soon destroyed by the damp Hebridean air, assisted by mice, and the neglect of his executors, if one can dignify with such a title the neighbours who, without legal obligation or sanction, moved in to burn the bedding after his death, so that a newly married couple could occupy the empty home.

But the love song he wrote to the woman who repudiated him, and, in doing so, repudiated all that he had believed in, as he himself came later to do, and which in fact the beloved herself never heard because she forbade him to sing it, still lives on. It is sung in Rona to this day, and in all the islands round about, by people who have long forgotten how it came to be composed, if indeed they ever knew. Just as his lament survives for the loss of the earthly paradise from which his people were driven but in which, if they had remained, they would almost certainly have died of hunger.

3

Blossom

In all the years I spent abroad I met only one man from Berisay. Perhaps this is not surprising because, so far as I am aware, I am the only Berisay man who ever found his way into the army in any of the South American republics. How that came about is a story in itself, but it is hardly relevant here. I may tell it some other time.

Anyway, I was in this city where there had been an earthquake followed by looting and rioting. We had been drafted in to restore order. Improvised camps were set up in the surrounding countryside, and the survivors were herded into them almost indiscriminately. It was not a situation in which you could stand on ceremony. I have never seen so much human misery in one place in my life, and, believe me, I have seen plenty here and there.

The first of the temporary buildings we erected was a prison. That tells you something about conditions in the city, and perhaps even more about the mentality of the people in charge.

Late at night I was speaking to one of my subordinates outside a row of ramshackle cells like rabbit hutches. They had no windows, just a hole in each door covered with wire netting. They were heavily guarded by soldiers with rifles at the ready, because a good push would have broken through

75

the flimsy walls, and we had rounded up some desperate characters in the course of the day. Desperate in both senses of the word: some of them were tough by nature, and no one can be tougher than your Latin Americans when they come that way, but others were driven to desperation by the plight in which they found themselves, and were quite as shocked as we were by the things they were doing. We had no time to sort them out: so far as we were concerned they were all there for the same offence, and they would all receive the same punishment.

I had just said "goodnight" to my lieutenant when I heard my name being called in an urgent whisper. Not my real name, but a name I had not heard for twenty years: my nickname as a boy in Seahaven.

"Mac an Babi! Mac an Babi!"

I don't know how my father came to be called "Babi". It may have been a corruption of "baby"—he was the youngest of the family—or it may have had something to do with Ali Baba and the Forty Thieves, or it may have come about in some other way I cannot even guess at. Anyway, as far back as I can remember, I was "Mac an Babi" to everyone I knew in the island of Berisay outside my immediate family, and especially to those who had grown up with me in the little town of Seahaven.

I thought for a moment it was a hallucination. The heat; the long hours we had to work; the horror of what we saw, and even more, of some of the things we had to do, had worn me out even in the few days I had been there. I stood stock still and said to myself, "God! Am I going mad?"

There was a vivid picture in my mind. So vivid I could have sworn I was looking at it with my eyes. Everything seemed completely real and quite external to me. I was observing an incident in which I knew I was about to intervene.

I was in a boat, a small boat, sitting at the tiller. Two of my boyhood pals were rowing. We were making for the Bagh Bheag where we were going to gather limpets. We were still in deep water but any moment, I knew, I would see bottom, and the shingle five feet below me would be as clear as if I was looking through a sheet of glass. The clarity of the water struck me particularly because it contrasted so sharply with the mud and misery around me.

There were two other boys in the bow of the boat, and suddenly they began to fight. God knows why, but it was a real fight. They had lost their heads completely and were hammering and clawing at each other like madmen. It was a dangerous situation in an unstable boat, and we were still far enough from the shore for someone to drown even although we could all swim like fish. I yelled at them. It was too late. One of them struck the other square on the chin and he went over the side. For a moment I thought the boat was going to capsize, but, as soon as it steadied, I jumped in after him: I could see that he was dazed and he sank like a stone.

Who was it I had saved that day? It was only when the question formed in my mind and was immediately answered I realised it was not a hallucination but a memory, and I had seen the whole incident in an instantaneous flash.

"Mac an Babi! Mac an Babi!" Again the urgent whisper, but this time I knew it was real, and I knew it was Blossom.

When I first knew Blossom he was the Artful Dodger, for reasons which were pretty obvious at times. We shortened

77

that to Dodger, and then to Jer or Jerry. Then, when the well-known boot polish first reached the local market, we extended it to Cherry Blossom, and, when we got tired of that, we shortened it to Blossom. Our progress through life from childhood until we joined the army is mapped out in my memory by the various stages in the evolution of his nickname. He was a central figure in all our ploys, and I can still date an incident by calling to mind fragments of the conversation and listening, as it were, for my recollection of the name we used for him then. It is odd how a nickname sometimes persists for life, or even, as in my own case, spans the generations, while others go through a series of trans-mutations before they really stick.

It was Blossom who was calling me. There was no mistaking the voice, although I had last seen him at Aldershot more years ago than I can readily calculate.

There was no one visible in the darkness of the camp, and the only other sounds were the tramp of the guard, and the lighter footsteps of my own lieutenant who was still within earshot although he had disappeared from sight.

I looked around, and then I saw Blossom, or rather I saw a vague white shape which I knew to be a face pressed against the netting of the nearest "window".

"I recognised your voice as soon as I heard you speak," he said as I went over to his cell, and, before I could reply, he asked me, "Do you remember the day you fished me out of the sea in the Bagh Bheag?"

The fact that we had both recalled the same incident at the same moment is no evidence of thought transference. The rescue was one of the high points of our long associa-tion as boys and it had a sort of perverse relationship with

78

the situation in which we now found ourselves sufficiently striking to bring it immediately into both our minds.

"Do you ever hear anything of the Tarbh?" he asked hungrily, as if news was the most important thing in his life.

It was the Tarbh who had knocked him into the water. He was well named "the Bull". He had a heavy frame, a thick neck, and a mane of reddish hair which flopped into his eyes exactly like a Highland bull.

"One thing sure," I said, trying to make light of the situation, "he's not likely to join us in this galley."

"Hell, no," said Blossom. "He became a parson, didn't he?"

"Yes," I said. "The last I heard of him he was the Moderator. There was a picture of him in the paper visiting a hospital in a sort of white lace front and these damn silly breeches the head parson wears."

"I could do with a parson right now," said Blossom, and that was almost the only reference he made to his own plight in a conversation which lasted far into the night. "There were times when I hated his guts," he continued, "but he was a good sort. I bet he remembers it too. He boasted often enough of the lander he gave me."

"Maybe he's sitting at a cosy fire right now in his manse in Edinburgh going over the same yarn with Calum Sty," I suggested.

"Calum!" said Blossom, with a great laugh. "He had one of the oars. How did he make out?"

"He became a doctor," I said. "He was in charge of the hospital the Tarbh was visiting. That's why his picture was in the 'Northern Star'. Two Berisay Boys Make Good."

"Damn it all," said Blossom. "You can say what you

79

like, we breed good stuff in Berisay."

There was real pride in his voice, and he said it as non-chalantly as if we were sitting in a pub, gentlemen of wealth and leisure, instead of standing in the dark, in a prison compound, on the outskirts of a stricken city, one on either side of a locked cell door.

"What are you doing here?" I asked him.

"Let's skip that," he replied. "I am here, and I'll take what's coming to me. Do you ever hear anything of Goosey Black?"

Goosey was the other oarsman. He was a doctor's son, not the son of a labourer like the rest of us, but it made no difference in Seahaven in those days. Indeed, if there was any difference between us, it was we who looked down on him, especially when we threw our boots aside in summer and went barefoot to save leather. His feet were white and tender and he suffered agonies trying to keep up with us as we scrambled over rocks or through the heather.

"Goosey was killed in the war," I said. "You must be completely out of touch with home."

"I'm sorry to hear about Goosey," he said, almost as if the death had just taken place. "Remember how he used to plan the raids on his father's fruit trees? He nearly went out of his mind the day his old man caught us and we accused Goosey of double crossing us, although we knew damn well the Tarbh was trying to light a fag and missed his warning signal. The old boy gave me a hell of a clout as I was shin-ning over the wall."

"I always seem to have been on the receiving end," he added a little wryly.

"Could you do with a smoke?" I asked him.

80

"God! Could I do with a smoke!" he replied, and I could see his fingers through the wire before I got the packet out. I gave him all I had but I had to pass them through one at a time because of the netting.

He lit one straight away and moved back from the wire so that the guard would not see the light, but we could still hear each other although we kept our voices low.

"I once caught thirty-seven mackerel hand running from the point of Number One," he said suddenly. "They were as thick as midges. I don't know anyone who ever caught as many."

It was obviously one of the great memories of his life. I had many happy memories, too, of days spent fishing from the slants and cross members of the piers but I had no recollection of Blossom's miraculous draught of fishes. He may well have caught as many as he said, but, whether he did or not, he certainly believed he did, and the very thought was sufficient to cheer him up for a moment and take his mind off the harsh realities.

He finished his cigarette and stamped on the stub. When he came back to the netting window he emptied his lungs of tobacco smoke with a deep sigh, straight into my face, not deliberately, but because it was so dark he did not realise how close we were. I coughed for a moment and he muttered an apology.

Then he said, surprisingly, "Do you remember the Rime of the Ancient Mariner? What was the name of the teacher we had then? Remember? We called him Murchadh Drawers? We passed his house on the way to school and there always seemed to be long johns on the clothes line."

His excitement rose with the recollection. "Every time we

81

came abreast of the garden, Goosey would point at the clothes flapping in the breeze and say 'there's a ship in distress over there', and we would all cup our hands around our mouths and yell 'ship ahoy', and then we would run like hell for cover."

I remembered well enough, but I was following another line of thought. "What brought the Ancient Mariner into your mind?"

"And ice mast high went floating by, as green as emerald," he replied, and I could hear our old teacher's intonation in every syllable although I could not say whether the mimicry was conscious or not.

"I have seen it," he said. "I was whaling for a few years. I think they were about the happiest years of my life. Since I grew up, anyway. Hard but plenty of booze and good pals. Many a tight corner they took me out of. And now and then I would meet someone from home and we would sit down for a pint and a blether."

"You know," he added quietly, "to talk of it is better than being there, in some ways at least.

"I knifed a man once. I don't believe in knives, but it was his own, and I stuck it in the bugger's back. We were in Fremantle at the time. You remember Cheesey from Toskavaig? His hands were all covered with warts and he had a red birthmark on his cheek, and we called him Cheesey because the birthmark looked like a tomato!" He laughed at his recollection of our curious boyish illogicality.

"He came into a pub in Fremantle where I was. Cheesey! We got cracking about the old days, and then he turned out his pockets to look for a bit of paper and a stump of pencil so that we could write down all the nicknames of people we knew in Berisay. God, what a night we had! At every name we would laugh like hell and start swopping stories, and have another nip or a pint or both to drink his health. The list was as long as my arm and, boy, were we getting drunk? And then this Dago started interfering. He wouldn't leave us alone. He wanted to know what we were laughing at and what we were writing. What the hell had it got to do with him? He argued that he had as much right to sit at the table as we had, and he could read and write as well as we could, and so on.

"Cheesey told him to get to hell out of it, and we went on with our work. And then out of the corner of my eye I saw him coming at Cheesey with this knife in his hand. It had a bloody great blade and a brass knob at the top of the handle which reflected the lights. I think that's what drew my attention. I gave him such a crack on the jaw he knocked three tables flying. I was barely in time. He had the knife in Cheesey but not deep enough to do him any harm.

"When I saw what he had done I pulled the knife out and stuck it in him twice. I left it in his arse. He was lying on the floor hollering blue murder when we ran for the door and the knife sticking up like a bloody lighthouse.

"I still have the list," he concluded abruptly. "You better take it. It's the only thing I have worth keeping."

I could hear him searching in his pockets, and finally he pushed a crumpled piece of paper through the netting. I put it in my pocket and thanked him, although I felt I could do without a grubby bit of paper that had been God knows where in the years since the pair of them wrote it in the pub in Fremantle.

"There's blood on it," he said. "I don't know whether it's

Cheesey's or mine. I skinned my knuckles on the bugger's chin. But it's good Berisay blood, anyway. It won't do you any harm."

We spoke for a long time about the boys who grew up with us in Seahaven. Bankers, policemen, shipwrights, plumbers, captains, doctors, ministers and God knows what. One of them was a Member of Parliament. I had kept in touch with them better than Blossom because my people still wrote regularly, and he lapped up greedily all the news I had until the darkness around us was peopled with shadowy figures: grown men we knew only by their names and their professions and their whereabouts—Canada, Australia, South Africa, India or Berisay itself—but at the heart of everyone of them a barefoot boy with corduroy trousers and a gad of herring in his hand, as we had known them in Berisay in the years before they became stereotypes in the gossip of distant friends.

"Is my sister Kate alive?" he asked at last and I had the feeling that he was ashamed to have to put the question.

"So far as I know," I said. "She's married of course."

"Yes, I heard that," he said. "What sort of bloke is he?"

"He's a stranger. I never met him. But my mother wrote me at the time. She said Kate had done pretty well for herself. There was a time when I might have married Kate myself if I had the sense."

"I wish you had," he said. "In one way. But if you had we wouldn't be here. You at any rate. I wouldn't have missed this for anything."

"There's not much I can do for you," I said. I was afraid he was relying on me to get him out of the mess he was in, but, even if I had got him past the guards, there was no way

84

out of the stricken city. He would be rounded up almost at once and re-arrested. There was no point in playing cat and mouse with him, and I think he understood.

"Robinson Crusoe was cast away on a desert island," he said. "That was bloody bad, but once or twice in my time I've been cast away in a great city and it's a damn sight worse."

When, at least, I left him, I bade him God-speed in Gaelic. We didn't use it much in Seahaven except to season our English slang but most of us had a smattering and somehow, in that situation, so far from home, it seemed to come nearer the heart than English.

"I think I'll have another fag," he said, and drew back from the window. I watched him light it up before I left.

As I walked home through the darkness I thought of the odd relationship that bound us all as boys and men. Even as boys we had different aptitudes, interests, and capacities. Some were brave and some were cowardly. Some were honest and others not. We had our likes and dislikes even within the group. Sometimes disliking became an almost irresistible hatred, and yet it was a hatred enclosed within a bond of affection, or at least acceptance, and, the further we got from home and the more casual our meetings, the warmer became the affection and the less we thought of the things which divided us.

Blossom was in his cell. I was going back to the best hotel in the city. Like the rest of the buildings, it was without light or water or sanitation but it was still habitable and in some respects luxurious. There could hardly have been a greater contrast between our situations and yet we were closer together in the things that matter, probably, than we had been as boys. We were certainly conscious of the fact that, however far apart we had grown, we were still branches of the same tree.

I lit a candle in my room and took out Blossom's list. You could see the writing get wilder and wilder as their orgy had progressed, but I sat up most of the night reading it. I lingered over every name to savour the bouquet and let my memories form. "God!" I said to myself, "it would be good to go back." And as quickly as the thought rose, I repudiated it. I had cut myself off irrevocably. There might still be a weal on my spirit where I had wrenched free from the parent stem, and, like a man who has had an amputation, I might sometimes have a sensation of discomfort in a limb that was no longer there. But going back would not restore it. It would only make me more conscious of my loss.

I folded Blossom's list as carefully as I could and put it in my pocket book. I had got over my distaste for the grubby bit of paper. It was now as precious to me as it had been to him, but possibly for a different reason. And there was the brown smudge he told me of which was Berisay blood although he could not be sure whose, and somehow I felt it was better not to know because the list had become the symbol of a brotherhood to which I had once belonged, a talisman that had come to me unexpectedly out of the past.

I did not go to bed at all. I had just finished my study of the list when it was time to groom myself as well as I could in the little drop of water my batman scrounged for me, thinking, as I shaved, how odd it is that in a stricken city a rescuer could have water to wash with while many of the victims he was there to rescue were still without any to drink. I thought that perhaps Blossom was better off in that respect as a prisoner than he would have been if he were still free to rummage in the rubble, among the rats and putrefaction.

Not that it mattered much for him, because I knew that, when the sun was up, I was going out to shoot him.

It is true I was not going to shoot him with my own hand but I was in charge of the firing squad detailed to execute looters. It was the toughest assignment of my life, and I still have nightmares about it, but I am glad that I couldn't pass the buck.

I am sure it made it easier for Blossom that there was a friend at hand, even in the firing squad. He certainly tried to make things easier for me. I forced myself to walk along the rank as the prisoners were blindfolded just so that I could have a last word with him. I didn't actually speak. I couldn't. But I put my hand on his shoulder and it spoke for me. Blossom smiled. A slow sad smile.

"Write Kate," he said. "Tell her I was asking for her."

I wrote Kate and told her that Blossom had died in the earthquake. I said I had spoken to him just before the end, and passed his message on.

Months later I had a letter from her, full of gratitude for all she imagined I had done for her dying brother, and particularly for letting her know that he still remembered her. The family had lost track of him for years: they knew he had gone to the bad, but he was still their brother.

I had the odd feeling that Kate, for all her love, perhaps because of her love, would have been less happy to hear that her brother was alive and to guess that he was struggling inadequately with life, than she was to know that he was safely dead, and that one Berisay friend, at least, had dropped a tear on his grave.

4

Requiem for Seonaid

David came to Berisay because of his interest in birds, especially the birds of cliff and shore. He had immense patience, and would lie on his stomach for hours, binoculars in hand, recording the movements of whatever species he was studying at the time, or just standing on the seafront watching the strut and by-play of seagulls on the harbour wall, when they manœuvred for a favourite vantage point or quarrelled greedily over a bit of fish.

"They're mocking us," he used to say. "The acquisitive society! One up on the Joneses! There you have it in the raw. The Almighty must have great fun sitting up aloft, unseen, tossing down bits of 'herring gut' and watching us scrabble in the mud."

It is questionable whether David believed in the Almighty, except as a cliché, a convenient symbol or loose bit of short-hand for something mystical which he did not understand, but which gave a meaning and purpose to life—if only he could discover what that meaning and purpose were. But when he had these discussions on life and death, or even a theory about some habit of the birds he was studying, he addressed his comments generally to himself.

Even in company he was the patient observer, saying little, but watching those around him as they played out their courtship ritual, or fought for the titbits of life, or just paraded in front of the rest of the company, preening themselves.

"We're a darned sight funnier than the birds," he would tell himself. "But if you watched the antics of human beings through binoculars you wouldn't be a scientist but a Peeping Tom."

His colleagues in the engineering firm where he worked were puzzled to understand what he and Bell could see in each other. She was practical, active, extrovert, always impatiently on the move, climbing the hills in fair weather or foul, swimming whenever the cold Atlantic water was half bearable, skiing in winter, or playing vigorous indoor games. When he screwed up the courage to take her to a dance, he sat in a corner of the room watching every step and flicker of an eyelid around him, while she took the floor with other men, coming back to him only for a few minutes in between. It wasn't very satisfactory for her but fortunately she never lacked for partners.

On the rare occasions when Bell slowed down for long enough to listen to him, and he shook off his shyness sufficiently to talk to her, she was enthralled. He had a lively mind and it was like a window on another world for her.

"I don't know why he bothers with me," Bell told her friends. "We're not in the same league intellectually. You have no idea what that lad hides behind his modesty."

They achieved an uneasy equilibrium. David became an immobile point round which Bell endlessly rotated, but she had to seek her recreation with other people, and David became jealous at times in a melancholy, acquiescent way.

She was impatient with him because she felt he was wasting his talent, lacking, as she saw it, an interest in the prizes within his reach. She was angry at times with herself for feeling neglected, and with him for making her feel that way, although she knew that he was anything but indifferent.

"This is hell," he told himself. "We will never come together, and we will never break apart. We will torment each other into the grave."

Bell thought the same, or at any rate felt the same, as she hurried from one social activity to another, gaining an added momentum from the fact that she was fleeing from an irritant which never ceased gnawing, although it generally lay below the level of conscious recognition.

It was David who suggested, in the bright June weather, that they should go off for a weekend in the hills. He discussed the idea with himself for weeks before he got round to asking her, and gave himself a dozen different reasons to justify his unusual decisiveness. At times, he persuaded himself that he could gradually learn to share her interest in outdoor sports, and hill walking seemed the easiest to start with. At times, he had erotic dreams about their weekend jaunt, but possibly his real aim, which he sometimes acknowledged to himself, was to try to win Bell over to his own interest in nature.

Bell readily accepted his invitation. "Thank God he's coming to the boil," she told her friends, but she had no idea whether she would accept him, if he did propose, or how she would respond if he sought a relationship less permanent than marriage.

Both of them felt that a weekend together would bring

90

them to some point of make or break, as indeed it did, although in very different circumstances from those they had visualised.

The sun was riding high when they set out, but there was a cool breeze which made walking pleasant until well after midday, and even then it was only in the gullies which trapped the sun that they felt any real heat.

The hill path rose steeply from the head of the loch and, by the time they reached the shoulder and began to turn inland, David was out of breath. He paused for a moment in the bend of the road and looked back.

"Half an hour's walk and here we are," said Bell, looking over his shoulder from her vantage point a few feet further up the rise. "Not a soul for miles around. Yet, look—across the loch you can still see the city. Isn't it wonderful to stand here looking down on it all, as if we were giants, and the people over there were pygmies, living in dolls' houses? On that side of the water houses, factories, schools, hospitals, museums and theatres. Everything! Industry. Prosperity. Civilisation. And on this side, a desert. A bare empty land, just the way God made it. And He made it right good. Smell the air, David. Fill your lungs with it. Isn't it wonderful to be able to escape so easily? No miles of jam-packed traffic to the coast : just 'over the hills and far away'."

David just grunted. They had both come from the south to live in the new oil town on the island of Berisay. City was too pretentious a word to apply to it, although, in using it, Bell had followed the common practice of the inhabitants, who liked to underline the contrast between Kinresort and the wilderness round about. Starting with a virgin site, the planners had made the most of it, using the irregularities of the countryside to create dramatic effects, so that every building which had any architectural merit was placed on an eminence but, when you walked up to see it close at hand, you found yourself looking back on a pattern of rooftops which seemed to be random, but which subtly led the eye to the loch and the hills beyond, giving the landscape scale without distracting from it. On the different levels one found a yachting marina, shopping precincts, open spaces, playgrounds, a cultural complex, all the facilities an urban centre could provide; and yet, there was the unspoiled countryside just over the wall, but now used for the first time by hundreds of town dwellers each weekend, instead of by a few wealthy sportsmen and impoverished crofters.

The early arrivals had lived through a hell of mud and hutted camps, but that was now behind them, and the town was visited by planners from all over the world; it had become one of the show places of Europe, Industry's answer to the environmentalists. But David was still dissatisfied.

"The valley of dry bones," he said at last.

"The valley of what?" asked Bell.

"It's a Biblical allusion," he replied. "It's the most magnificent skeleton of a town ever devised by man, but it's still waiting for someone to breathe into it the breath of life."

"You can fill your lungs with the breath of life," said Bell sharply. "When did you ever breathe anything sweeter or purer?"

"We are very lucky, Bell," he agreed. "But I can't help feeling that God is a biologist, not an engineer. He doesn't work with blueprints, but with living cells. The more we succeed in planning our environment, the less chance we have of clambering on to the next summit on the march of evolution."

Bell had no time for David when he began philosophising. Life is good, so what the hell! "Come!" she said to him sharply. "It's time we were clambering on to the next summit on the march to dinner."

They picnicked by a stream, resting their backs against the buttress of a broken-down bridge, built many years ago by a wealthy sportsman for his ponies as they carried him to the hill or brought back the carcasses of the stags he killed. David had given a whoop of joy when he saw the bridge. "That's the sort of ruin I like," he said. "A fitting memorial to an age that is gone and not lamented."

"I knew you would like it, and I was determined to get you here in time for lunch," said Bell, as she shared out the sandwiches.

"I've been extravagant," said David, producing a bottle of Beaune from his haversack. "I want to pour out a libation to the souls of all the stags who perished here to slake the blood-lust of the idle rich." A swirl of wine, like a fleck of blood, rotated beside them for a moment before it was sucked into the current, and disappeared. "And now a toast to ourselves."

It was certainly not for the libation he had brought the wine, and not wholly for the toast. He hoped that it might loosen his tongue and help him to say to Bell what he had said to himself innumerable times and in innumerable ways when he wooed her in his mind, which he somehow found more satisfying, as well as easier, than wooing her in reality.

They lay in the sun for a while and talked about their respective childhoods, as if each was trying to weave the

93

other into the pattern of the past, so that, when eventually they came together, it would not be a meeting of strangers linked by physical ties, but a reunion of two old friends who retrospectively knew each other from childhood, although they had never met until chance brought them to the same office in the fabrication yard at Kinresort.

When at last they rose, Bell shivered as if a cold wind had touched her—or a premonition. They had been so close to a decision, but David had not spoken, although at that moment she would unquestioningly have said 'yes'. She set off at a cracking pace to cover her annoyance—or to show it—and quickly outdistanced him. When she paused to watch some deer on the slope high above them and David caught up with her, she said to him with a bite in her voice, "Poor little David! Is he hot and bothered and out of breath?"

"He is just that," said David crabbedly. "And even if you're not, there's no need to gloat. You got the genes that make for long legs and strong thighs. I didn't, but you can't claim any credit. It just came out of the lucky dip."

"Like your brains," said Bell. "Or are they different? There are times when I could murder you."

Their voices were rising and, for the first time since they met, they were really quarrelling. David was rapidly losing control of himself when Bell broke off the argument and resumed her progress while he hurried after her shouting incoherently and getting more and more out of breath.

Suddenly Bell stopped. "Look," she said, and pointed in astonishment to a little cottage in a sheltered valley, high up on the mountainside but overlooking a little bay. There was smoke coming from the chimney and, as they watched,

94

an old woman came from the house with a pail of slops and emptied it down the hill.

"I didn't know there was a village here," said David, his anger gone and his interest aroused.

"There isn't," said Bell drily. "I've been here dozens of times and I've never seen a village."

"You didn't see the house until today, if it comes to that," said David.

"You can miss a single house but not a village. I've been all over these hills and there is no village," she said firmly.

By this time David was striding as rapidly as he could towards the old woman. He wanted to know how and why anyone continued to live in such remoteness when there was a town not far away where life was assumed to be so much more comfortable.

"Welcome to Ard Bheag," said the old woman. Blackened by peat smoke and wrinkled by age, her skin was almost as tough as the mud-caked boots she was wearing but, as she spoke, her eyes lit up and a gentle smile spread across her face, warm and mischievous, like a summer sky reflected from the surface of a deep dark pool.

"I would like to explore that smile," David told himself, as he held out his hand to her.

"We don't see many visitors here," said the old woman. "Just one or two passing through in the summer with packs on their backs, like Christian with his burden. I wonder if they ever get rid of them?"

"You live here all alone?" asked Bell, as she joined them.

"Not alone," replied the woman. "It's a big village, this. Do you know, when I went to school there were more than eighty children in Ard Bheag. What fun we had and you never saw such strong men and handsome women.

"Just like myself," she added, with a smile. "Every family had its own croft and its own boat, and cattle and sheep on the hills. And dogs. You never saw so many dogs in your life. It was a busy place at harvest time or when there was a fank on, or when the shoals of herring came into the loch. But they're all dead now. All dead. Except my brother."

"I told you there was no village," whispered Bell. David paid no attention.

"Your brother lives with you?" he asked.

"Yes," said Seonaid. "He's in the house now. He'll be sitting in his chair just inside the door. He sits there all the time. Old age doesn't suit him. He's deaf and he won't speak to me. Not even to answer when I speak to him. He just sits there, looking. He's there when I get up in the morning, and he's there when I go to bed at night. Looking straight in front and not saying a word."

David was puzzled. "He goes to bed after you and gets up before you, and spends the whole day just sitting?" he asked.

The old woman's smile opened again, fuller than before. "It's none of my business whether he goes to bed or not," she said. "I'm only his sister. If I was married to him I could tell you that."

"But he never moves out of his chair as far as you can see?" asked David, but before she could reply Bell cut in brusquely, "I don't see why we're bothering about these things. It's no concern of ours."

David waved her aside. "There are no young people in the village at all?" he asked.

"Lots of young people," said the old woman. "This was

96

the happiest village in the whole wide world."

"I mean now," said David. "Today! Are there any young people?"

"I'm the youngest in the village now, and the oldest too, apart from Angus," she replied.

"Angus is your brother?" asked David, gently trying to prise the fact from her confusion.

"Yes," she said, unexpectedly flaring up. "And you would go a long day's march before you would find anyone lazier. He wasn't always that way, but now he won't cut the peats or go to the well or milk the cow or shear the sheep. He won't even bank the fire or shut a window for me."

As the woman rambled on, David became conscious of Bell's growing irritation, but he shrugged it off. This was more interesting even than his beloved birds.

"You mean that you do all the housework and the cooking, and milk the cow as well?" he asked.

"We haven't got a cow," she replied. "Or sheep. I couldn't manage that. There's not much housework to do and, as for cooking, a cup of tea is all I want."

"But what about Angus?" asked David. "You've got to cook when there's a man in the house."

The old woman looked anxiously over her shoulder as if to make sure that she was not overheard. "He's a worry," she said confidentially. "If I say to him, 'Angus, would you like a kipper or a herring or a piece of sea trout from the burn?' he'll just look ahead and say nothing." Then she laughed, as she added unexpectedly. "I don't know what I would do if he said 'yes' because we have no kippers now, or herring, or sea trout from the burn. Nothing but shop bread and jam, and maybe a tin now and then. We didn't have tins when I was young."

David could not have been more interested in the old woman if he had discovered a creature from some remote period of pre-history still surviving in the heart of a modern city. She was a complete anachronism within a few miles of the new town of Kinresort but, he felt, she was also a problem, so that his compassion was engaged as well as his curiosity.

Bell was rapidly passing from impatience to real anger, but his mind was so fully occupied with the old woman he missed the danger signals.

"Do you never feel lonely here with no one but your brother, summer and winter?" he asked.

"Why should I?" replied the old lady, her face lighting up again with an ineffable smile. "Who could have better neighbours? There's Calum John, and Annabel and Bocan and the Sprat. The schoolmaster never passes the door but he comes in for a ceilidh, or the minister. And there's all the young folk, just like yourselves, forever quarrelling and making love. Dancing and singing by the lochside in the moonlight, and coming in on dark nights to ask Angus about old times in the village, and the fairies and the fishing. And even when I'm not fit to go to church myself I can hear the psalms coming up from the valley below. You never heard anything sweeter in your life, with all the voices rising and falling together like the sea."

She paused as if she was listening, and for a few minutes she was so completely wrapped in her own imaginings she forgot the existence of her two visitors. Bell took the chance. "Come," she said, grabbing David quite roughly by the arm. "There's no village and there's no psalms. There's nothing down there but the derelict houses with the windows gaping and the roofs fallen in, and a few rotten planks lying on the beach where the boats used to be. I've been there often and often, although I've never stumbled on this little nook in the hillside before."

"Just a minute," replied David, refusing to let himself be dragged away.

"I won't 'just a minute'," snapped Bell. "We're wasting the day."

"I know," said David, "and I regret it just as much as you do, but she needs help. My guess is that her brother needs it even more."

"You are the most exasperating person I know," retorted Bell. "You've been pestering me for months to marry you, although you've never said a word. I'm sick to death of your dumb eloquence whenever we meet. I've given you the chance of a weekend together to see if you can be decisive for once and make your mind up, to say nothing of mine, but what do I find? You're far more interested in a crazy old woman than you are in me!"

"That is bad luck for both of us," said David, "but how are we going to feel if we go away and do nothing? One of these days she may be found here, dead."

"We'll all be found dead one of these days, if it comes to that," said Bell. She swung around and set off, back along the path by which they had come, with a step which said more eloquently than any words that the weekend was over, and much else besides.

"I left him once," said the old woman gently, while David still swithered whether to run after Bell or not. "I left him in a tiff. He wouldn't make up his mind. I told him I didn't want to see him again, ever, and I left him in the middle of a dance. Right in the middle of a reel. I can see them now in the barn with a stable lamp hanging from the rafters. Everyone swirling and screaming and laughing, and the melodeon going until you thought it would burst. I didn't dance with him again that night although he asked me thrice, and I danced with every other boy in the village. I was never so proud or so pleased in my life. There he was pleading with me, and there I was longing to throw myself in his arms. When the dance was over it was high tide, and we all went down to the beach to help them launch the boats. The sea was calm and the moonlight was spread across the water just like butter. It was so still you could have walked along it like a golden stairway. I blew a kiss to every boat except his. I was longing for him, but I was pleased that I was hurting him. Before daybreak there was a gale from the north, and flurries of snow. I never saw him again. Or my father, or my two uncles that were in the boat with him."

She paused for a moment, looking into an immense distance, and then she put her hand gently on his arm. "Don't worry. Wait! Just wait! If you have patience, she will come back to you. If life permits."

David himself was quiet for a moment or two. He was hurt by her story as if her loss had been his own, but his real fear for his own affairs had been diminished. They spoke for a long time about old days in Ard Bheag and the old woman's mind seemed quite clear then. David came back to something which had been puzzling him for some time. The old lady had spoken of bread and tins, but how did she get them in such a lonely spot without even a road? When he put the question to her, she smiled at his simplicity.

"Murdo takes them to me," she said. He still looked puzzled. "You know Murdo?" she added, as if jogging his memory and chiding his forgetfulness. "Everyone knows Murdo, the postman."

David was surprised that a postman visited such a lonely spot, but the old woman assured him it was so. "Murdo comes twice a week," she said, "and he takes me all the messages I want. A little tea and a little bread, and he brings me a letter every week."

It was a relief to David to learn that she received letters. He assumed she had a son or daughter, a nephew or a niece, someone who would take responsibility for her when she finally got past caring for herself, which could not be very long, but she assured him that she had "no one living in the whole wide world, except Angus".

When he began to question her about the letter, she told him she got two different kinds. One came with money in it. "Not much, but enough to pay Murdo for the things he buys me." The man who wrote them came to see her once or twice. "An impudent man," she said, "forever probing and prying and asking questions." David was relieved to know that the Social Security folk had some loose contact with her, and he pursued his enquiries about the other letters, about which she was very mysterious.

"It's a very funny letter," she said, "and it comes every week. I never saw one like it before. But it's good of him to write. Every week without fail! I tie them up in bundles with a ribbon and pretend they're from a daughter or a grand-daughter, and she's coming to see me in the summer. And she'll take me away from the wind and the rain, and the cold and the wet, and the long dark nights in winter, and

101

the peats to cut, and the hens to feed, and the sheep I have on the hill. She's a lovely girl and she has the bonniest children. Three of them. Two girls and a boy. The boy hasn't gone to school yet, and he'll take his granny for little walks in a bonny place with the sun shining and trees and water."

As she spoke, she retreated into her remoteness once again, but suddenly the present came back into focus as she turned directly to David and asked, "Would I be his granny, or his great-granny?"

"Tell me more about the letters," said David gently, and she rummaged in the pocket of her apron and took out the latest of them.

It was a circular from Littlewoods!

"I have hundreds and hundreds and hundreds in the house," she said, "but I always carry the last one with me."

David was puzzled to know what to say to her, but he finally decided that he must handle the situation in her own terms. "This is from Littlewoods," he said.

"Do you know the man?" she asked eagerly.

"I never met him, but I know of him," said David. "He's very wealthy and his place is in Liverpool. He writes every week to thousands of people."

"That's kind of him," said the old woman, and then she added wistfully, "I wonder if any of them are as lonely as me?"

"Many of them are lonelier, even although they have people all around them," said David. "Loneliness isn't something that comes on you from the outside.

"The loneliest people of all are those who carry their loneliness about with them," he added and, as he spoke, he thought a little of himself.

102

"I replied to him once," said the old woman. "I didn't write the letter myself. I'm not up to writing letters now. But I asked Murdo to write and tell him it was good of him to remember me. I should have done it long ago, but I didn't think."

David smiled to himself as he wondered what the staff of Littlewoods made of Murdo's letter, but he did not comment. He tried instead to persuade the old woman to let him get a doctor to see her brother in the hope that he might do something for his deafness. "It would make a great difference to you if you had your brother to talk to."

Her reaction was quite unexpected. She was angry. "I don't think he wants to hear what I say, and that's the truth," she said. "It's a bad thing when your own flesh and blood fall out with you."

Her anger passed quickly and she put her hand on David's arm again. "Perhaps if you spoke to him, you could knock a little sense into him," she said. "I'll make a cup of tea while you're talking to him. We can have it out here in the sun, like we used to do at the peats, when the whole village was out together working in the bog."

"There'll just be the two of us," she said, giggling with mock coyness. "Your girl will be jealous.

"But go and talk to him now," she added, pushing David towards the porch. "You'll find him sitting in there staring into nothing."

She bustled off round to the kitchen door, intent on making a cup of tea, while David walked reluctantly across to the porch, wondering what on earth he could say to a deaf old man. As he opened the door, the stench stopped him in his tracks and, peering into the half light, he could see a figure slumped in an ancient armchair, dead, and visibly rotting.

He shut the door hurriedly and backed off into the fresh air, just in time to receive a cheery greeting from Bell, who came hurrying down the path again.

She had expected David to follow her and, if he had, she would probably have resisted any attempt to make the peace. But when she found herself striding on alone her anger had time to burn itself out, and she began to wonder whether David might not have been right: they did have an obligation to the old woman if there was anything at all they could do to help.

David had remained behind, full of compassion, but puzzled what to do. Bell had no difficulty in choosing a course of action once she decided to help. She left the rough track which led back to the town and struck straight up the mountainside, checking her position from time to time from her map. On the shoulder of the hill, above the path, there was a mountain bothy with a small radio transmitter for use in emergencies. She got through quickly to the police: gave them a rough outline of the situation, and asked them to make arrangements to have the old woman removed to a hospital or Home.

She also suggested the advisability of having the cottage destroyed. She did not have David's reason for thinking that way, but she had formed the impression that it was primitive and unsanitary and she did not want it left as a temptation to storm-bound hill walkers who might shelter there. Although Bell escaped from the town to the wilderness whenever she could, she liked to have her wilderness organised and equipped with the sophistication of the town, but discreetly, so that the illusion of wilderness and the pleasure of being out of doors were not destroyed.

As she returned to the path, Bell kept a sharp lookout for David. She had not seen him pass, but she could have missed him. She deliberated for a few moments and then decided, with an inward smile, that he was almost certainly still fussing over the old woman, wondering what to do. This sense of her own superiority as a manager sent her hurrying gladly back: she must take David under her wing as she had taken the old woman—he was so very helpless and so very lovable.

"I'm glad you're still here!" she shouted, as she approached. "There's help on the way. I've been to the mountain bothy and phoned the police."

"Good God, we don't want the police!" said David. He didn't know what exactly he wanted, but he felt that the old woman's integrity, as he called it, should be protected from prying eyes. Get her into a Home by all means, but gently, by persuasion, and without destroying the world of illusion in which she lived, a little sadly and meagrely perhaps, but with greater contentment than many much more prosperously endowed.

"You're a ditherer, David," said Bell, but it was kindly spoken, with reconciliation in every inflection of her voice.

"Where is she?" she asked.

"Making a cup of tea," said David.

Bell sprung into action. She had a vision of David, and possibly herself, being asked to drink from dirty tea cups with Heaven knew what ill effects.

"I'll help her," she said, making for the porch.

David barred her way. "She'll manage without you."

"No doubt she will," said Bell, "but I want to see that the crockery's clean." Much to his surprise and delight, she then kissed him on both cheeks and added, as she brushed him aside, "I don't want to lose you the day I got you."

Before David had recovered his poise, she was in the porch. She came out white and retching. "Good God, David," she said. "It's far worse than I imagined."

"You see now why I don't want the police," said David.

"You're a great big soft-hearted cuddly baby," said Bell. "Diddums not want the police." But when she saw that David was getting really angry she added quickly, "Look, David, she's mad. Quite mad. She needs help—and control."

"Maybe," said David grudgingly. "But I don't want policemen crawling all over her. They'll trample her into the ground with their great flat feet. She's mad and sane at the same time, like most of us, and I want to see her leave here with her dignity and her dreams intact, even if it's the last thing I ever do."

"See, I have three cups. I knew you would be back," said the old woman, coming up unseen behind them. She was holding the lid of a biscuit box in her hand in lieu of a tray, with three cups of tea and a plate of buttered scones.

"She did know you were coming back," said David aggressively, as if he were still defending the old woman's integrity against Bell's policemen.

A difficult period followed, with the old woman pressing them to drink her tea and eat her scones, which David attempted with some loathing although he did find, once he got a piece into his mouth, that the scones were delicious. Bell did not even make the attempt, but David was relieved to see that she was careful to conceal the fact that she was

106

pouring the tea on the grass beside her, and crumbling her scone beneath a stone.

Then the old woman began to coax Bell to go and see her brother. "Angus might speak to *you*," she said, adding with a warm laugh, "He always had an eye for the girls." She laughed even more heartily as a new thought struck her and she added, "I don't know what would happen to me if he went off and married you."

"We will arrange for a doctor to come and see Angus. It would be nice if he could speak to you," said David, seeing a chance of preparing her for what was about to happen.

She made no immediate response, but some time later she raised the question herself. "You really think a doctor could do something for Angus?"

"I'm sure of it," said David, with a sidelong glance at Bell, as he thought of the horror in the porch.

"How will I get a doctor?" said the old woman helplessly. "Many a time I wondered what I would do if Angus fell ill, and I had to get help in a hurry."

"I have sent for a doctor," said Bell, and David blessed her inwardly for the gentleness with which she said it.

The old woman laughed. "I don't think she's wise enough," she said, giving David a poke in the ribs. "How could she get a doctor when she's hardly been out of our sight?"

"I phoned the police, and asked them to get a doctor for Angus," said Bell, trying to assimilate her own action to the tactics David was trying to pursue.

The old woman shook her head. "Worse and worse! Where could you find a policeman here? There hasn't been one in Ard Bheag since the climber fell and broke his leg.

And that was years and years ago. It was before Angus quarrelled with me. He helped the policemen with the stretcher. He was older than any of them, but stronger. He's a strong man, Angus, especially when his dander is up. That's why you have to be careful what you say to him."

She broke off excitedly, pointing to the path. "There's someone coming, and it's not the postman. It's not Murdo's day, and it's not his step.

"I'll go and make some fresh tea. He'll be thirsty, whoever he is," she added, as she hurried into the house.

"It can't be the police already," said Bell, as she looked at the speck on the horizon and wondered how the old woman could be so sure at that distance that it was not the postman.

David meanwhile had been studying the approaching figure through his binoculars. He handed them to Bell. "What on earth do you make of that?" he said, and she knew that he was speaking from puzzlement rather than surprise.

Bell studied the approaching figure for a few moments. "If it wasn't too crazy for words," she said, "I would say he's a commercial traveller."

"That's what he looks like," said David. "What on earth is anyone doing out here dressed for paved city streets and spivvy bars?"

"He's even got a brief case," said Bell. "He's just dropped it. He's in a bad way." By this time, she was on her feet, hurrying to meet the stranger. David followed.

As soon as they were within hailing distance the stranger shouted to them, "Am I on the right road for Ard Bheag?" He was hot and weary and muddied about the face, where he had rubbed the sweat with hands which had obviously been in contact with the ground when he had stumbled on the steeper parts of the path. He was wet to the knees, or even higher, having waded the river which Bell and David had jumped. He limped heavily and Bell had a vision of the raw red flesh inside his city shoes where the stones had gouged his unprotected feet. "He's reached Ard Bheag," she said to herself, "but he'll have to be carried out of it."

When David told the stranger that he had actually reached Ard Bheag, he was obviously relieved, but he was quite glad to accept an arm from each of them along the last few hundred yards to the spot where the old woman was busy re-laying the picnic in preparation for the new arrival. When he learned that Bell and David were strangers to the place like himself and that the only resident was the old woman, 'granny', as he called her, he was dismayed.

"God Almighty," he said, "Do you mean that she's Mrs. Seonaid Macrae, Ard Bheag?"

"I have no idea," said David. "I never heard her name, but she must be, if there is such a person, for certainly there's no one else."

The stranger mopped his brow and sat down. He surveyed the broken-down cottage, and looked back at the path along which he had come. He was obviously unimpressed by the glory of the hills, and the freshness of the air. "Why does anyone live in a God-forsaken place like this?" he asked. "If you can call it living."

No one replied, and the old woman handed him a cup of tea, and some scones. "I'm sorry I haven't an egg in the house, or I would boil you one," she said. "You must be hungry after your walk."

"Hungry!" said the stranger, with a laugh. "I was a young man when I set out this morning, but look at me now. Ready for burial. I feel as if I had spent half my life on that bloody goat track."

David warmed to him. A man who can laugh at his own predicament quickly makes friends. The old woman took to him too. He was eating her scones with relish, having had nothing to eat on his long walk, unlike David and Bell, and not having quite so much reason as they for repugnance. Bell was still puzzled, and a little wary.

"You're from Littlewoods," said David at last, satisfied that he had solved the mystery.

"She knows she's won?" said the stranger, indicating the old woman.

"She doesn't even know she's tried," said David.

"What's all this double talk?" demanded Bell.

The old woman had gone into the house for some more scones, so David had freedom to explain to Bell about the old woman's letter of thanks to her correspondent. Presumably, he suggested, the postman, when he was asked to write to Littlewoods, wrote in the way Littlewoods were accustomed to, rather than the way the old woman had in mind.

"We had a telegraphed claim in Miss Macrae's name," said the man from Littlewoods. "Then we had a phone call from a man who said he represented her. He said he would take me out to her if I came up. When I got to Kinresort I found he had landed in hospital. Appendicitis or something. I saw him for a few minutes and he offered to try to get me another guide, but I said I would manage fine. He warned me it was further than I thought, but he gave me directions, and here I am." He looked a little ruefully at his feet. "And here I remain! I'll marry the old girl. We can live very happily on this," and he took from his wallet a cheque made out to Miss Seonaid Macrae, for just over a quarter of a million pounds.

The man from Littlewoods, who now introduced himself as Spencer, made a formal little speech to Seonaid congratulating her on her win, and then handed her the cheque with a flourish. She quite clearly did not know what he was talking about and, when she took the cheque, she turned it over and over, studying it with obvious puzzlement, and then turned to David—"What is it?"

"It's a cheque, Ma," said Spencer. "Money. The stuff you buy the groceries with."

"Is he making a fool of me?" asked Seonaid, once more addressing her question to David, as she handed the cheque back to a bewildered Spencer.

David explained to her that it really was money, and it had come from her friend Littlewood. But why was he sending money to her? She had never asked him for any. "He was so pleased with the letter Murdo sent for you," said David. "He's giving you a quarter of a million pounds."

"How much is that?" asked Seonaid.

Spencer and Bell began together trying to explain to Seonaid what she could do with a quarter of a million pounds. Spencer wanted to tell her about the service his firm could give in the way of investment advice. Bell was anxious to coax her into an old folks' Home in town, by telling her that she was now independent and she could pay her way and engage maids to look after her, and have all the luxuries she so obviously lacked.

111

"If I go away to the town, who'll make the breakfast for Angus?" asked Seonaid.

"Don't worry about Angus," said Bell. "We'll take him too." As she said it, she looked across at David but he was lost in thought.

It was ironical, he thought. Obscene. What had money to do with Seonaid Macrae and her problems? What had money to do with anything that really mattered in life? "If she was buried in snow as she's buried in money," he muttered, "she might freeze to death, but she wouldn't be corrupted."

Spencer meanwhile was trying to rally her. "You'll have all the money you want for the rest of your life," he said. "You know, Ma, all the boys will be after you when they hear that you're rolling in it."

"The only boy I ever cared for is out there in the sea, drowned dead," said Seonaid. "I don't need money, and I don't need a home in the town. Murdo brings me the pension every week and I'm happy where I am." She rose, as if she wanted to break off a frivolous conversation, and walked into the house with as much dignity as her years and rheumatism had left her.

Each of the three saw the situation differently but, before they could begin to discuss it, they heard a low drone and a helicopter appeared over the brow of the hill, followed by a second and a third.

Spencer was puzzled by this development; Bell was relieved; and David was angry. His anger mounted when he saw that the third helicopter was loaded with pressmen and television crews.

As quickly as the police and the ambulance men got out

of the first helicopters and assembled their gear, the reporters were in action, recording every move in the rescue, and even providing a running commentary by radio link, so that the housewives in Kinresort, and throughout the country, as they hoovered the floor or prepared the evening meal, were entertained to a dramatic account of the discovery of an old woman alone in the hills, 'Old Mother Crusoe', as one commentator dubbed her, dying of neglect and starvation until the welfare services swooped in from the sky to carry her back to comfort and civilisation.

When a microphone was thrust in front of David's face, he swore and pushed the man aside. Bell too was disconcerted. She believed there was no other way of handling the situation, but she was sorry for the old woman's sake, and for David's, that there was so much fuss, although she comforted herself, and tried to comfort David, with the thought that the old woman would not know that her affairs were being discussed in a grotesquely distorted form in every home in the country by people who didn't give a damn whether she lived or died, or whether she had ever been born.

"It's all so bloody impersonal," said David. "She's no longer a woman, but just a peg to hang a story on."

As for Seonaid, when she heard the helicopters, she hurried out of the house shouting to her visitors, "There's someone hurt on the hill! I'll get blankets. Come and help me, David." She used his name as if he were a lifelong friend.

Before she reached the house the first helicopter had landed, and she changed her mind and hurried over to the policemen. "I'm sorry I haven't cups to go round, and the condensed milk is finished, but if you wait till I've washed the dishes, I'll make you some tea."

Bell took her by the arm and led her gently aside, explaining that she wanted to have a private word with her. "You fill them in, David," she said, indicating the police.

David went across to the senior officer. Immediately, the pressmen and the camera crews crowded round. It was at this stage David pushed one of them aside. The officer signalled to a constable and the reporters were motioned back, but they paid little heed, and David finally took the officer on to a rock where they could talk privately for a few minutes without eavesdroppers.

The reporters now switched their attention to Bell and Seonaid, swarming round them like midges. Fortunately, Bell had succeeded in persuading Seonaid that she must go with her in one of the strange flying machines if she was to get a doctor for Angus. Seonaid thought it would be a rare adventure for a cailleach like her to be away up in the air like the eagle, and she look Bell's arm and walked with her towards the nearest helicopter, talking gaily about the surprise Angus would get when the doctor came and he suddenly began to hear again.

"Deaf as he is," she said, "you would think the noise of these things would have brought him to the door."

Spencer was in his element, in spite of the aching feet. Here was publicity such as he had never dreamed of, and he hobbled around among the reporters, brandishing the cheque and giving ever more dramatic accounts of his efforts to persuade Seonaid to accept it.

"Dammit," he told the listening millions over the radio link, "I don't think she knows what money is!"

The effect was rather spoiled by the fact that Seonaid, at

that moment, shook herself free from Bell, just as they were going into the helicopter, and hurried across to Spencer, saying, "I forgot the money," and holding out her hand for it.

When he had given her the cheque, a little reluctantly because he had no time to organise some appropriate ceremonial, she turned to the reporters and, although she did not know it, to the world outside, and explained, "It's not mine, really. It's Murdo's by right. The man would never have sent it if Murdo hadn't written the letter."

"Who is Murdo?" demanded the reporters, thrusting the microphones even closer into her face. Seonaid did not know what the microphones were but thought it all very improper and very rude.

"Fools," she said. "You don't even know who Murdo is!"

She had taken a dislike to the men who were harassing her, and that made it easier for her to go back to Bell, and get on board the helicopter. Bell explained that Murdo was ill in hospital. "Poor Murdo," said Seonaid. "I'll go to see him, and bring him the money. Won't he be surprised?"

The helicopter took off immediately they were on board, followed by panning cameras and the cackle of commentaries.

Attention was then turned to Seonaid's house, where charges of explosive were being placed to blow it up. The police were going to search it but David dissuaded them. "It's a shambles inside and there's nothing of value there, absolutely nothing."

"You've been through it?" asked the police officer doubtfully. David said he had, and spoke as if he was familiar with every nook and cranny.

The police officer looked at his watch. Time was getting

on. "Right," he said. "Go ahead with the demolition."

The reporters protested. They wanted interior shots, and material for graphic accounts of the conditions under which Old Mother Crusoe had lived alone while the world passed by on the other side of the hill. The police officer said he would give them ten minutes. He looked at his watch again.

By this time David was standing by the plunger, which was already wired to the charges.

"Look!" he shouted, "if anyone goes into that house, I'll blow it up with them inside."

He was determined to protect Seonaid's privacy and dignity, but he could also see awkward questions being asked of himself if the body was discovered. Would any policeman understand or believe his reason for lying?

The reporters paid no attention to David. They went swarming towards the house. The policeman was also now determined to make a search, but he made first for David.

He flung himself forward, bringing David down with a rugby tackle, just as the reporters poured into the house, and David fired the charge.

The explosion was heard in innumerable homes throughout Britain, followed by total silence, until a studio announcer suavely covered the hiatus with a comment about technical difficulties, and the listeners' attention was switched to other matters as a new programme came on.

Bell saw the house disintegrate just as the helicopter crossed the summit of the mountains. "Good old David," she said to herself. She knew there had been no time for a police search; she had not seen the reporters go in, and she assumed that David had succeeded in concealing the old woman's grisly secret. She was glad for his sake.

But by that time, David was under arrest, and the police were already beginning to puzzle over the extra body found amid the debris.

Their work went forward, unimpeded and unobserved by radio, press or television, as silently and as privately as Seonaid's own life had sped.

5

Jonah on Rousay

The schoolroom was empty when the party from the town arrived. It was a desolate setting for a concert.

"How on earth are grown men and women going to squeeze into these benches?" asked Mrs Pat Saunders. She was familiar with the Usher Hall in Edinburgh and St Andrew's Hall in Glasgow, and elegant city assemblies in private houses, but her husband was now the resident surgeon in the little cottage hospital in Seahaven and she was doing her best to adjust to island living, and to help her husband's work by raising funds for the hospital. So much equipment was desperately needed.

It was she who suggested forming a hospital concert party to tour the rural areas of the island, and those who thought they knew it better tried to discourage her. Apart from the inevitable resistance to any new initiative, they had a genuine fear that the villagers would not respond to concerts organised from the town, and an even greater fear that the ministers would disapprove and the hospital would lose the very generous support it got, without effort on the managers' part, from the local churches. But Mrs Pat was not easily discouraged. Small and plump and round and rosy-cheeked, she had the resilience of the rubber ball she so much resembled. "She may be a bantam," said the hospital chair-

118

man, "but she rolls over you like a tank." It was before the era of bulldozers, and the first world war was still fresh in the memory.

When she looked at the empty schoolroom with patches of black mould where the damp was creeping through the dreary green and brown walls, the few pathetic pictures torn roughly from illustrated magazines, the blackboard still bearing the traces of a half expunged lesson in arithmetic, and the paraffin lamp on the teacher's desk, sizzling and smelly and leaving the corners of the room in murky darkness, she feared for a moment that her advisers had been right. But only for a moment.

They had decided to commence the concert tour in Loch Scriven, the most remote village from the town. Although now linked with the rest of the island by road it had, until comparatively recently, been accessible only by boat and it still had many of the attributes of a small self-contained remote island.

"It's as far behind Seahaven as Seahaven is behind the mainland," the hospital chairman had told her in an attempt to prepare her for the shock in store. But, if she remembered his warning when she looked round the schoolroom, she dismissed it briskly from her mind. "Where's the bell?" she demanded.

"We have no bell," said the headmaster, a timid little man who was known locally as the Cailleach, which means an old wife, but in this case was actually a shortened form of the Gaelic name for the owl, bestowed on him not because he kept watch all night, which he didn't, but because he slept all day and, according to village gossip, never more so than when taking a class. He disliked work and disliked worry and would gladly have consigned Mrs Pat and her entourage to the deepest pit in hell, but for the obligations of hospitality which compelled him to welcome them when they arrived and invite them to partake of supper in the schoolhouse at the end of the concert. The supper had been prepared with loving care, and with no reluctance, by his wife, who was glad to have the monotony of her existence relieved by the presence of strangers, even for an hour or two on a Friday night.

"Who ever heard of a school without a bell?" demanded Mrs Pat. "How do you summon your pupils?"

"We have a conch," said the Cailleach.

"A conch!" she exclaimed.

"A sort of a shell," he explained, drawing it vaguely with a movement of his arm.

She thought it most peculiar of the islanders, more peculiar in fact than anything she had yet encountered, to summon the children to school with a sea shell. She did not quite understand how it could be used for that purpose, but she was determined that, if it could, it would also be used to summon her audience together.

"May I see this conch?" she asked. The Cailleach had no intention of letting her do anything so *outré* as blow the school conch at that time of night, but her momentum was much greater than his inertia and he scuttled away obediently at her bidding.

He returned with a large convoluted shell rather like a ram's horn in shape but delicately patterned in cream and pink and brown. "A sailor is supposed to have brought it home many years ago," he explained as he handed it to her. She took it but seemed uncertain what to do.

"You blow it like this," he said, taking it back and putting it to his mouth like a bugle. It produced a surprisingly deep and powerful note, which contrasted with his own small stature and lack of forcefulness.

Mrs Pat took it from his hand again and strode to the door, although strode is not quite the right word: her determination was revealed by her expression and the gestures of her arms; her legs were too short to stride. She raised the conch to her lips with the obvious intention of blowing a blast which would bring the dead as well as the living scurrying from the village to the schoolhouse gate.

"It was the funniest thing I ever saw in my life," the Cailleach told his wife later in the evening, in a rare moment of animation. "She blew till I thought she would burst, and she didn't make a 'beek', not a bloody 'beek'."

"Blow me a blast," said Mrs Pat to the Cailleach with a voice like a sergeant-major. He took the conch, then hesitated. His fear of making a fool of himself in the eyes of the villagers was even greater than his fear of the martinet at his side.

"They'll come all right," he said apologetically. "We don't believe in clocks in Loch Scriven. Not on this side of the water, anyway."

"You will!" said Mrs Pat emphatically and, she believed, prophetically.

"More's the pity," said the Cailleach, with surprising firmness. "I'm hanged if they had clocks in the Garden of Eden."

Mrs Pat made no reply. She was not particularly interested in the Garden of Eden, and her fear for the concert was relieved by the sound of talk and laughter somewhere in the darkness, and obviously moving towards the school.

In twos and threes people drifted in, chattering in Gaelic, of which she understood not a word, a fact which added greatly to the sense of adventure and missionary achievement with which she saw herself carrying the torch of musical culture into Loch Scriven in support of modern medical science.

"Civilisation attacking barbarism on two fronts at once," she told her husband when she got home that night. "A pincer movement. Give me time and I'll drive them out of the trenches yet." She did really see herself engaged in a crusade: middle-class Edinburgh, in shining armour, on a white steed, scattering the powers of darkness on the uttermost fringes of the Gaelic world.

As soon as the room was decently filled, she gave the signal for the concert to begin, although stragglers were still arriving and almost every item was interrupted, or half drowned, by the noise of clumping boots and whispered greetings which offended her city sensibilities, although even she became gradually aware of the warm spirit of good-humoured, gregarious conviviality which filled the room so palpably that you could almost see it. The evening, much to her delight, but largely in spite of her efforts, was proving a great success. It was the first formal concert ever held in Loch Scriven, the locals were treating it as an impromptu ceilidh on a grand scale and, like an atomic bomb, where the critical factor is mass, the programme threatened to explode at any moment into an uncontrolled manifestation of communal high spirits.

The start was slow, however. Mrs Pat herself opened the programme by singing "Flow Gently, Sweet Afton" and

"The Lass of Richmond Hill". She sang well but the dolts just sat and gaped at her—as she put it herself on numerous occasions afterwards.

Then one of the hospital nurses sang a Gaelic traditional song, unaccompanied, in a thin mournful voice, and the audience began to thaw. Mrs Pat was not in the least bit envious of the applause which greeted the nurse: the fact that (as she saw it) the people of Loch Scriven had no musical appreciation merely emphasised the magnitude of the task she had undertaken in setting out to civilise them.

In the course of the evening the Cailleach whispered to her, "That's Groucho". He indicated a man who had just come in. Mrs Pat had never seen anyone quite so lugubrious. He looked as though the dough hadn't risen when the good Lord made his face, and his limbs were so loose one expected them to fall from the wires at any moment, like buttons from a breaking thread.

The Cailleach must have read her thoughts. "He needs tightening at the back like a badly laced corset," he whispered. The shaft of wit from the dreary schoolmaster surprised her until he added, "It's one of his own cracks".

"Who's Groucho?" she asked.

"Just Groucho," he replied. "Ask him to sing."

"Sing!" she replied in amazement. After a severe surgical operation he might be fit to heave coal, she thought; but singing was a spiritual exercise. It never occurred to her that there was very little suggestive of the spiritual, or even the artistic, in her own roly-poly plumpness.

"He's great. There's no one in Loch Scriven to touch him," persisted the Cailleach.

Mrs Pat did not doubt that, but she did not regard it as

123

a recommendation. However, the evening was now going well and, in deference to local feeling, she announced that Groucho would sing, an announcement which was greeted with tremendous hilarity and applause. The applause was a tribute to Groucho's popularity, the hilarity was occasioned by the unexpected use of the nickname by the posh lady from the town.

"Mr Mackenzie," whispered the Cailleach, but Mrs Pat did not trouble to retrieve her mistake, and in any event Groucho was already on his feet and launching into a song.

He didn't smile. There was no visible change in his expression. Yet, as soon as the first note sounded, the whole audience lit up with mirth.

If Mrs Pat had been as perceptive as she was sharp, she would have realised that behind the gawky frame there lurked a great comic spirit. Instead, she assumed mistakenly that the audience were laughing at the singer's ungainly posture and tuneless singing, as it was to her unaccustomed ears.

"This is one of his favourites," whispered the Cailleach. "He gives me hell in one of the verses."

Mrs Pat heard the words, but missed the import and decided that she had failed to catch the schoolmaster's whisper. The idea of a local jester singing his way through twenty verses in which everyone in the village was lampooned, including the minister, the schoolmaster, and the district nurse's philandering cat which, according to the singer, gave her more confinements than the whole population of Loch Scriven added together, was too remote from her experience to understand, even if it had been explained to her in detail and, if she had understood the nature of the song, she would still have been baffled by the schoolmaster's placid acceptance of a situation which set a roomful of his recent pupils laughing their heads off at Groucho's description of his foibles.

But the schoolmaster was wrong in one particular. Groucho was singing his favourite tune right enough, but he had new words to it, words he had composed since coming into the hall, in which the visitors from the town were described, dissected and hung on the line for everyone to see in all the curious splendour of their Sassenach idiosyncrasies.

It was done so good-humouredly that the audience, even as they laughed at Mrs Pat, came to accept her, and to hug her to their bosoms like a cuddly doll. From being an utter stranger she passed straight into village folklore, thanks to Groucho's wit and, although she did not know it, she would never be a stranger in Loch Scriven again.

She was now, to the local people, 'one of the folk we can laugh with', and in truth she was laughing uncontrollably, although she would be hard put to it to say why. The drollery of Groucho's expressionless face was part of it, but only part; the laughter around her was so infectious she would have been carried away even if she had been blind.

When the schoolmaster, with such diplomacy as he could muster, explained to her over supper in the schoolhouse, what the laughter had been about, she was not offended. The concert had been a triumph, and she was riding high.

"You mean he made all that up on the spur of the moment?" she asked.

The schoolmaster suspected that Groucho had been mulling over the event for days, and had most of his ammunition assembled in advance, even if he did add some last-minute touches to give it an air of spontaneity, but he felt he would not do serious damage to the truth by replying in the affirmative, and when Mrs Pat got back to town she deived her unbelieving neighbours for days with her account of the skill of the 'natives' in impromptu compositions 'in honour of their guests'.

"That is something I must find out more about," she said on more than one occasion, and when Mrs Pat found out about things she did it thoroughly, although generally her vigour was greater than her understanding. The results of her enquiry, however, lay a little in the future.

After the concert, Groucho spent the night with his girl friend. Perhaps it would be more truthful to say with one of his girl friends. He was popular with most of them because of his wit, which was enhanced by the deadpan inexpressive face. In the dark, of course, they could not see his face, but that was an advantage in another way because it gave them a chance to forget that he was so surpassingly ugly. None of them thought for a moment he would ever marry, and none of them had any ambition to take him on.

Groucho was a rolling stone, and they all knew it. He had been a seaman, a shipyard worker, a miner in British Columbia, a whaler in South Georgia, and a farmhand for a time in Perthshire, which was the most unlikely job of all for a crofter from Loch Scriven. Now he was at home, weaving intermittently, and his earnings depended on the infrequent conjunction of two variables: the availability of work, and the will to do it.

The brother with whom he shared a miserable thatched house on the outskirts of the village was even less attractive for any girl who wished to marry. He was gaunt and sallow with a nose so thin that Groucho said he sharpened pencils on it, and there was always the suggestion of a drip from the point, so that it became celebrated in song as the only well in the village that never ran dry. He looked consumptive, and probably was, and, unlike Groucho, he was a recluse, and so neglected his appearance that he became known as the Hobo.

Some of his history was known to his fellow villagers, but only some, because there were aspects of it beyond their range of interest or even comprehension. He had studied for the ministry, but took to drink. That was the beginning and end of it so far as his neighbours were concerned, but the Hobo was much more complicated than that.

He was a brilliant classicist, and when he went to university, he took up the study of modern languages as a hobby for which he neglected his prescribed subjects, failing repeatedly in examinations which would have been child's play if he had taken the slightest interest in them. He would probably have had to leave the university in any event for want of funds, but the war intervened, and in the mud and blood of Flanders he lost what little ambition he had to be a Highland minister, and acquired a violent hatred of war, injustice, and above all the English upper classes.

These hatreds were confused and compounded by his hatred of his own people for what they had become. In his view, they were docile serfs, touching the forelock to sporting landlords, and letting themselves be manipulated by doltish, arrogant ministers in the name of a God who did not exist.

"Hell!" he used to say. "There's more spunk in the sheep.

127

At least they've kept their language, they say 'baa, baa', as they did at the dawn of creation. But we have thrown our language away. Oh, yes, we still speak it in Loch Scriven in a sort of a way, but every year it gets thinner and thinner, like watery gruel. Instead of acquiring new words to express new ideas, we go on repeating the same old platitudes in words that would disgrace a baby. For God's sake, we're now using English words for words we already have, and we still call it Gaelic. If the buggers had cut our tongues out they could not have made a better job of it!"

It was not often the Hobo indulged in outbursts of this sort since coming back to Loch Scriven because he seldom spoke to anyone except his brother but, from time to time, mysterious strangers came to see him out of his old life in the city; but even they were repelled by the fact that he insisted on speaking in Gaelic or, if that did not suit them, in French or German. On principle, he never spoke a word of English.

In fact, he carried his hatred of English so far that he never read the modern British poets until he could get them in a French or German translation. Occasionally he compromised to the extent of cadging an American edition, telling himself in self-justification, "The buggers may have written it but at least they didn't print it."

His particular hatred, oddly enough, was Hugh Macdiarmid. They had almost everything in common except language. "English is bad enough without bastardising it," he would declare. "I'll kiss him on both cheeks when he gives up Lallans and writes in Gaelic. But, let's face it, the Lowland Scots have done us a damn sight more harm than ever the English did."

The Hobo did as little work as possible. He lived by poaching, which he took up on principle rather than for any pleasure he got out of it, and by sponging on his brother, which was a pretty threadbare existence: like a thin grey lichen trying to find sustenance on the face of an even greyer rock.

But he read and wrote incessantly.

On the morning after the concert, Groucho was surprised to find him busy at the back of the house stuffing their "borrowed" peats into canvas sacks.

"What the devil are you doing?" he asked. The fact that the Hobo was exerting so much physical energy was in itself almost as surprising as the use he was putting the energy to.

"I am getting the boat ready," was the reply.

"For God's sake, if you're going to be mad, at least be mad at the right time of year," said Groucho.

The Hobo had been speaking off and on for months of leaving Loch Scriven to make his home on Rousay which was little more than a pinnacle of rock thirty miles out in the Atlantic. A small population had once maintained a precarious existence on Rousay mainly by birds' nesting: the cliffs were so precipitous that even fishing was impossible, except on rare days in summer. Twice, at least, within the period of written records the population of Rousay had been completely wiped out by famine or disease and although, after the earlier disasters, the island had been reoccupied by landless crofters, it was finally abandoned nearly seventy years ago because the sheer drudgery of existence was more than human flesh and blood was prepared any longer to endure. If anyone could survive on Rousay it was certainly not a man who shirked physical exertion like the Hobo and spent his time with books.

"What the hell do you want to go to Rousay for, anyway?" asked Groucho.

"To find the source," said the Hobo. "The first people who lived on Rousay were missionaries of the Celtic church. They were refugees from a crumbling civilisation, just as I am. They kept a little cruisie alight, according to their own beliefs, during a long night of darkness. The walls of their chapel are still standing. I will roof them over and live there. Like Noah of old, I will send out a dove from time to time to see whether the floodtide of greed and barbarism and inhumanity is subsiding. I will come back when I know that a few isolated peaks of sanity are beginning to appear somewhere on the face of the earth.

"You know," he added, "the Flood had nothing to do with water. That's all poetic symbolism. The so-called civilisation of Noah's day drowned in its own bloody vomit. And that's what's happening to us."

"If you go to Rousay you won't drown in your own vomit, that's pretty certain," said Groucho. "Your stomach will be too damned empty."

"My work will keep me going," said the Hobo. "We need to find a way back to the simplicities of life, when it was whole and balanced. That's what my poem is about. I'm tired of all this trashy, introverted self-cannibalism which passes for literature today. I am writing a new gospel that will ring down the ages like a golden bell."

"And you're writing it in Gaelic so that no one can bloody well see through you," said Groucho.

"It's the message that counts, not the language," said the Hobo. "If a man has something worth saying people will

130

read it even if it's in Swahili. Look at Pepy's diary. If people will break a code for bloody gossip, what will they do for the secret of life?"

"Bugger all," said Groucho drily. "Why did you come back to Loch Scriven if you're so keen to run away from it?"

"I'm not running away; I'm carrying the search one stage further. We used to know the secret of communal living here, but we have forgotten it."

"You won't find much communal living in Rousay," said Groucho. "There's nothing there but birds—and rats."

"I have to get back to first principles," said the Hobo. "I want to drain my mind of all the false values and notions and ideas I have acquired over the years. As a people, we have been bruised and battered by history. The continuity of our development has been broken. The only way to get on to the right path is to go back to the point where we lost the way, and start again.

"I hate this place and I hate the people and they hate me," he continued, "yet I'm the only man who really cares for it. Of course they romanticise it, like a man on a bed of nails singing the pleasures of his couch. Of course he doesn't want to change anything: he daren't even roll over. The only way to make the bloody thing bearable is to lie like dead. And that's what they are in Loch Scriven. I'm the only man among them who cares sufficiently to tell the truth. I want to see them get off their bloody nails and live.

"You're the worst of them," he added, turning savagely on his brother. "I listened to you last night, outside the schoolhouse door, prostituting your talent to give them a false sense of pride and superiority, making fun of the poor truaghans who strayed from the city fleshpots into a situa-

131

tion they don't even begin to understand. We don't need an anodyne. Pain is our only hope. Instead of oiling the wheels, you should help me to tear the bloody place apart and begin again from scratch."

"Look," said Groucho, serious for once, "we can only eat the bowl of gruel life has put before us. If I add a little salt to make it palatable I'm doing more for my fellow men than any saint or sage or seer who ever got the poor buggers bogged to the neck in bloody nonsense pursuing a will o' the wisp."

"Give me a hand with these sacks," said the Hobo. He despaired of getting his brother to share his views or his aspirations, or even to begin to understand the poem he was working on.

"I'll do a lot less," said Groucho. "You'll get no one in the village to help you. They'd be glad enough to see the last of you, but they don't want your blood on their hands.

"This is no time of year to go to Rousay," he added. "You could never even land. Nine days out of ten there will be green seas breaking half across the island. You know as well as I do that no one has ever landed there between October and May and, even in the summer, you have to choose your weather well."

He turned on his heel and made for the house. The Hobo went on filling his sacks with a savage intensity. He knew that Groucho was right and, although he sweated over his useless task until nightfall, he said nothing about going to Rousay again for more than a year, and then it was Groucho who first raised the matter, driven to desperation by Mrs Pat, and the love of the minister's daughter.

At first he was flattered by Mrs Pat's attention. She came

repeatedly to see him, accompanied by Macdougal, the Gaelic master from the school in Seahaven. He was an un-imaginative stirk who specialised in Gaelic because competition was less keen than in the other disciplines and he was fit to specialise in nothing else. His knowledge of the language had the precision and pedantry of a computer. He spewed out facts without any understanding of their significance, relationship, origin or consequences: neither his natural ability nor the schooling he had received had programmed him to handle facts—the living tissue of experience —in any other way than as inanimate fossils.

For hours on end Mrs Pat quizzed Groucho about his compositions, getting him to sing them again and again while Macdougal noted them down. She tried herself to record the tunes, but her equipment for the task was limited, and she forced them into a mode of music with which they had no affinity.

The end result was a grotesquerie. The tunes were disembowelled and had nothing left but the mummified skin. The poems were translated into English with a verbal precision which strewed the words around like pebbles on a beach: hard, isolated, unrelated, grinding against each other in dissonance and incoherence.

Still, she got it published, in a lavish edition (at her own expense) and earned a considerable reputation in the popular press as a folklorist rescuing imperishable gems from the midden heaps of a dying culture.

She sent Groucho a copy, specially bound in fine leather, with an effusive letter of thanks. The pale blue binding with a Celtic pattern delicately tooled in gold was no more incongruous in the broken-down shanty where Groucho received it than the contents were in relation to the original, but the original was the work of art, her translation the shambles.

Groucho admired the craftsmanship of the binding, turning it over and over in his hand to study every minor detail of the design, but when he dipped into the contents he dropped it hurriedly. "God," he said, "there's as much life here as in a slab of butcher's meat."

But if there wasn't life, there was dynamite. One or two copies of the book in the standard binding found their way to the village. No one discussed the quality of the translation, few were really competent to do so, but everyone who read it realised that the village was now standing naked before the world, their warts, their pimples, and their private parts all ruthlessly exposed.

The book sped quickly from hand to hand and, with its progress, the anger grew. No one blamed the real culprit. Mrs Pat was dismissed as a poor ignorant creature who had strayed in from the uncomprehending English-speaking world outside, but Groucho was one of themselves and he had betrayed them.

Groucho had no idea when he recorded the songs that they would be published, or even that they would be translated. If he had known, his author's pride might still have led him astray, but he was able honestly to proclaim his innocence. Unfortunately, the more he protested, the less people believed his disclaimers.

Almost overnight, he became as bitterly hated as he had been greatly loved. No mockery bites sharper than that which exploits the traits for which we mock ourselves. Self-mockery, in private, can reinforce the identity of the community even while it cauterises the worst of its sores, but mockery in public, by an outsider, destroys the confidence of the victim and, paradoxically, reinforces his resistance to change. All the malevolence which Mrs Pat engendered was concentrated on Groucho's head, because nothing is ever stamped on with so much vehemence as a fallen idol.

Groucho was denounced from the pulpit by big Hector Maclean, the local minister, a martinet who kept his family under a discipline so severe that they almost lost touch with real life. The attack from the pulpit did not worry him at first, he rather enjoyed the notoriety, but then he became aware that people were avoiding him: not only the elders and communicants but the young as well, and even the girls he had been friendly with.

As he walked through the village, he became aware that people coming towards him turned suddenly into the crofts to look at a beast which did not require attention, or hurried up to a neighbour's door which, he felt certain, they had intended to pass by. And at night, when he went to one of the usual ceilidh houses, instead of being welcomed and having an honoured place cleared for him he quickly found himself alone by the fire except for the host, who could not very well leave his own house, but found other ways of showing that the visitor was not as welcome as he used to be.

Groucho found isolation much harder to bear than the Hobo, who was by nature a solitary, although even he pined at times for company, especially the company of women. The distance between the Hobo and the other villagers developed gradually, and the initiative was his own. He often regretted that he repelled people but he was so prickly he repelled them again whenever the chance arose of a reconciliation. His longing for companionship could be more intense, in some ways, than his brother's because it was seldom or never gratified, but he could only maintain his integrity by making a virtue of his self-imposed cross, and he had the solace of creative work. It was always in his blackest moods the words began to sing.

"I need my cordon sanitaire," he used to say when Groucho tried to entice him into the company of women. It was lightly said, but sometimes he would add with deeper feeling, "You lucky bastard! I need one too, but I was born a puritan." And that's what he was in a very real sense: a man who rebelled openly against the repression of the community by the church, but bottled up his own instincts in the same explosive way.

Groucho lacked the inner world the Hobo could retire to. His talent was more superficial; he was dependent on social contacts to give him the victims for his satiric wit, and he needed an audience with laughter and applause to give him a purpose in composition. When the doors of the village were slammed in his face he was hurt, angry—and bereft.

It was in this situation Peigi, the minister's daughter, first came to visit him. He was surprised when she opened the door of their ill-kept house and came in with an odd mixture of timidity and brazenness, but he probably understood why she had come better than Peigi herself and the Hobo, in spite of his remoteness from his fellows, had a deeper understanding of the situation than either of them.

The brothers were both at home when she called but she paid no attention to the Hobo and he took no part in the conversation.

"I thought I would come round to see if there was any-

thing I could do for you," she said. "I brought some scones."
She produced a small shopping bag which had been hidden
under her coat and took from it some freshly baked scones.

"Where can I find the teapot?" she asked. In a short time
she was nervously taking charge of the house, preparing an
evening meal, and tidying up the indescribable mess in which
the bachelor brothers lived. She did not stay long but, as
she left, she said to Groucho, "I'll come again to see how
you're doing," almost as if she were speaking to an invalid.

"A filly that's never been harnessed can't kick over the
traces," said the Hobo when she had gone.

"Meaning," said Groucho, "that she's kicking because she
has been, and too tightly at that."

"Yes," said the Hobo. "It's always close to the tyrant the
plot is hatched."

"Why did she come to us?" said Groucho. "That's what
I can't understand."

"She didn't come to us. She came to you," said the Hobo.

"I've never spoken to her in my life," said Groucho. "She
never gets out of her father's nunnery except to go to church,
and she won't see me there."

"That's the whole point," said the Hobo. "She knows your
reputation, and she's curious. She wants to play with fire.
Now that you're a leper she can come like an angel of mercy.
She's got to hide the fact of her coming from her father and
her mother, but with your martyrdom as excuse she can hide
the purpose of it from herself as well."

Peigi was not the sort of girl Groucho would have stopped
to look at if he met her in the village with half a dozen
others but when she came to him, night after night, in secret,

137

bringing him gifts of food, and once a pair of socks she had knitted for him, and when, although perhaps she did not herself realise it, she enticed, or dared, him to walk her back to the manse through the darkness, she became a torment past bearing.

"I will laugh like hell when you hang up your hat in the manse," said the Hobo, who began for the first time to take an open interest in one of his brother's affairs and tease him for it.

"I like her scones," said Groucho, trying to laugh it off, "but you know damn well I could never marry her." Then he laughed immoderately—"God, they would skin me alive if I did!"

"You don't need to marry her," said the Hobo.

"That's what's worrying me," said Groucho. "She's that damn stupid I would never forgive myself for taking advantage. I wish to peace she would stay away."

Although he knew the battle his brother was fighting with himself, the Hobo was surprised when Groucho reopened the question of Rousay, and offered to go with him for a few weeks until things blew over.

"Fleeing from the siren with wax in your ears," he taunted.

"It's not the siren I'm thinking of," said Groucho, "but all these damn fools that won't have me in their houses now. If I'm out of sight for a few weeks they may open up their doors again when I get back."

When the two brothers got busy preparing for their expedition there was great merriment in the village, and numerous cryptic references to the Ark, although in this case no building was necessary, merely the provisioning of the vessel for a stay on a windswept island where there was neither food nor fuel.

They left at night, partly to avoid the attentions of the village children but, more importantly, so that they would arrive with first light, and have a full day unloading stores and preparing their shelter. In the long Hebridean twilight there was no real darkness, and as they pushed off, they saw a slim figure hurrying down to the cove where the boat had been moored. There was no mistaking her.

"If we don't hurry, we'll have a lodger," said Groucho, giving the boat a vindictive push from the slipway with an oar. He seated himself on one of the thwarts and rowed briskly for a few moments to take the boat out of hailing distance from the shore, before letting her drift while they set the sail.

The brothers were silent until they got the boat properly trimmed and out into open water, but they could still see Peigi on the shore waving excitedly.

"Thank God I got out of that before any damage was done," said Groucho, as they rounded the point and began to lift with the long groundswell from the open ocean, the last dying echo of a violent storm which had spent itself hundreds of miles to the westward. Knowing that he was too far away for the gesture to be seen, Groucho blew Peigi a mock kiss, before lighting his pipe and settling down with the tiller tucked under his oxter.

The Hobo was quiet. Unnaturally quiet even for him. He did not reply to his brother, and made no comment on his gesture. But then, he had a lot to think about, because only he and Peigi herself, knew that the damage was already done.

Groucho had tried to avoid her and slipped off to walk around in the darkness on the evenings he thought she was likely to call, and thus, to the excitement of sneaking from the house without her parents' knowledge, for an illicit purpose, was added the frustration of being rejected by the man for whom she was running the risk. Her visits became more frequent as she became more frantic.

When she came to the house and found that Groucho was out, she was impatient to be off. The Hobo was unattractive in himself and his reputation in village gossip was sinister in a different way from Groucho's. Besides, she had quieted her conscience with the assurance that the two brothers were always present when she called, an assurance she found comforting even when she was tempting Groucho to walk her home.

One night when she found the Hobo alone and turned towards the door, he began to recite a poem. It was a love song written to herself: a song of great power and beauty. She listened until he finished and then left.

A few nights later, when he began to recite another love song to her, she didn't wait to hear it. She fled. The Hobo was touched to the quick by her obvious dislike of him. He hurried after her into the dark and finally came up with her not far from her father's manse which stood apart from the village by a little loch with a few conifers around it, teased threadbare by the never ceasing wind. There they struggled until she finally succumbed.

The Hobo was both jubilant and ashamed. He tried to look on the incident as an act of justice, poetic justice, executed on the minister and all he stood for, through his daughter, but he hated violence, even non-physical violence

140

like the minister's dominance over the minds of his parishioners, and he cursed himself for destroying his own integrity.

"She's lost her virginity," he told himself, "so what? So have I. Her body has been breached, but I've suffered in my soul. Besides, the bitch could have shouted for help, and didn't, but there was no one within earshot I could call to."

The Hobo thought a lot about the incident on the way to Rousay. He tried to analyse his own complicated state of mind and Peigi's, and the parts played by Groucho and the minister, as well as himself, in creating the predicament in which the girl was placed. He listened in his mind to a dialogue between an all-seeing God who had foreordained the rape from the beginning of time for His own inscrutable purpose, and a blind scientist with a dice box in his hand, who said life was like water pouring over a cataract, and what happened to the little bits of human driftwood caught up in the flood was all a random chance, and didn't signify: they would all inevitably reach the sea, but why the sea existed or the cataract or the flotsam was inexplicable and irrelevant; there was nothing real but the forces that bound them together and the statistical laws which proportioned the chance. It gradually shaped itself into a poem, different from anything he had ever written. On the surface it was bawdy, almost scatological, but all his self-loathing was there as well, all his frustrated desire for communion with his fellow men, and the realisation that, because of his own warped nature, the things he most valued in life were only worth striving for as long as they were unattainable.

His silence was unbroken until they reached Rousay and began nosing towards the only cove where a boat could be held at anchor, and that only so long as the wind was in the east and did not freshen. All their stores, food, peat, paraffin, tarpaulins to make a shelter, fishing lines, and snares for the birds, mounted on long bamboo canes, and even a few live sheep, had to be manhandled on to a narrow ledge of rock and then hauled up a narrow path to the top of the cliff.

When fishermen from Loch Scriven occasionally went birds' nesting on Rousay, they hauled the boat with block and tackle up the cliff face clear of the swell, but that was more than the two of them could manage. Groucho was on the ledge, examining it to see whether there was any other way in which they could secure the boat for a week or two until they were ready to return but, as soon as the last of the stores had been landed, the Hobo gave the boat a push seaward with his foot, quite deliberately, and jumped ashore to join him.

"What the hell did you do that for?" demanded Groucho, making a wild but unsuccessful attempt to catch the boat.

"You're not tired of Rousay already?" said the Hobo with a malicious grin.

"No," said Groucho, "but I will be before long, and so will you. I mean to have a few good nights in Loch Scriven yet."

The Hobo laughed and pointed to the boat, now gripped by the ebb tide and moving rapidly away.

Groucho was afraid both for his own safety and his brother's sanity, but there was nothing he could do but take the lead in making a habitable home in the old ruin where a hermit had lived and worshipped many centuries before in circumstances perhaps similar in some respects, but very different in others, to those which brought the brothers to Rousay. By nightfall they had contrived a roof of sorts and lit a fire, although the wind still whistled through the gaps in the drystone wall, and they were frequently disturbed by the arrival of petrels, whose nests were in the walls and who resented their eviction after an occupation which had lasted hundreds of years.

For some time after the brothers left, their disappearance was a matter for merriment in Loch Scriven. Everyone knew where they had gone, and everyone expected them to come back thoroughly chastened. But when they failed to return by the time the equinoctial gales blew up, the villagers began to worry. If they did not get off soon, they would be there for the winter. And there was a possibility that their boat had already been smashed to matchwood.

A rescue operation was mounted, at some considerable risk, but it failed of its purpose. When the crew sighted Rousay they could see Groucho clambering down the cliff face to the cove to meet them, but the Hobo remained above. As they edged in between the fangs of the rock, Groucho tried to throw them a line, but the Hobo hurled down stones from the clifftop which threatened to smash the boat or kill his brother. They shouted at each other and both of them shouted at the boat's crew but it was all confusion, and in the freshening gale it took all the fishermen's skill to get the boat safely out of the cove again.

Several further attempts were made, but winter came early that year and it was quite impossible to effect a landing. On the last occasion, it was not even possible to approach the island as there was a northerly gale blowing, with flurries of snow. Nothing at all was seen of the two brothers, but the fishermen reported that smoke had been rising from their

143

shelter so presumably they were still alive.

In the long dark winter nights one of the principal topics of discussion round the ceilidh fires in Loch Scriven was the strange story of the two brothers, and every time the wind blew up there was deep concern for their safety. Even in church, the minister prayed for them, and without rancour.

As soon as the weather was fit in the spring, long before the time at which boats would normally have ventured to approach Rousay, a crew composed of all the ablest skippers in the township set off, and the whole village gathered at the slipway to see them go. Never had so much seamanly skill sailed out of Loch Scriven above a single keel. They were unable to land at Rousay but they circled the island several times as close as they dared. They signalled and shouted and used every means they could think of to attract attention but they saw no sign of life.

That night, several of the elders walked across the hill to Seahaven to invoke the aid of the police. A Fishery cruiser sailed for Rousay with a doctor and the procurator fiscal as well as policemen and coastguards. The weather was still rough but, unlike the smaller fishing boats, the cruiser was able to lie off the island until a favourable conjunction of wind and tide made it possible to get ashore.

When the landing party reached the hermit's cell it was open to the sky: the tarpaulin had been carried away by the winter gales, but the brothers were there, both of them dead.

Surprisingly, Groucho had been the first to succumb. He was lying by the hearth with a blanket spread carefully over him. The Hobo was seated beside him in a chair roughly

144

fashioned from driftwood, as if he had just nodded asleep by the fire. At his feet was a piece of driftwood, carefully notched to record the days. Deeper notches marked the Sundays, which the people of Loch Scriven took as a sign that the Hobo had been "converted" before his death, although from the fact that the Sundays were marked right from the start it appeared that it had been merely a convenience to make it easier to reckon the weeks. There was one mark much deeper and longer even than the Sundays which appeared to record the date of Groucho's death, because after that the notches became shallow and shaky as the Hobo's strength had ebbed. No one could be sure precisely when he died, as he might have survived for a day or two after he had lost the will, or the power, to make another mark.

The bodies were taken back to Loch Scriven for burial, and the brothers were quite genuinely mourned. Even the Hobo was missed, as a village landmark would be missed if it suddenly disappeared while Groucho, until they turned him out, had been part of the living heartbeat of the village. Big Hector Maclean preached a powerful sermon on the frailty of man, both physically and spiritually, but the villagers noticed a compassion in his voice which had been lacking before and which they attributed to the humiliation he had suffered when, a few days before the discovery on Rousay, his daughter had given birth to a child, refusing vehemently to tell him the father's name.

"It was my fault, and it's my problem," she said in reply to every question.

Mrs Pat was thrilled by the story of the brothers' deaths: it was so dramatic, so very Celtic, or Viking, or something.

145

She was even more thrilled when her husband handed her the Hobo's notebooks. He was the doctor who had gone to Rousay, and no one had demurred when he took possession of a few rain-sodden jotters.

There were six slim books in all, written in a small spidery hand, with numerous erasures and corrections. A long Gaelic poem described the Hobo's search for his own identity, not as the isolated individual he was, but as part of a community living and growing and changing, just as he was living and growing and changing, but according to a rule and rhythm of its own. There was a lyrical description of the physical geography of Loch Scriven, but its purpose was not so much to celebrate the beauties of the landscape as to explore the effect of various natural pressures on the society in which he was nurtured, and there were heroic passages in which he adventured into history in the same way, trying to assess the events which still echoed through the folk culture, long after the facts had been distorted beyond recognition or completely forgotten. He studied the place of the church with surprising tolerance, setting against its deadening influence the fact that, more than any other agency, it had helped to keep the language alive, which he regarded not only as a banner and symbol of his people's identity but its vehicle as well. He also wrote with great felicity and insight of the part the church had played in creating a new, although a harsh and hateful, bond to hold the community together when the older bonds, derived from the clan, were destroyed by the centralising state, both Scottish and British; the callous frivolity of the chiefs, rioting their substance away in London; and the greed of the new masters who came in to carry through the Clearances.

146

Perhaps the most valuable books were the final ones, in which he tried to apply his experience, or rather his observation, of a small community, for he stood aloof from it himself, to the predicament of industrial man. In close, convoluted, allusive language he attempted to project the Gadarene path of western civilisation, and to argue that salvation lay in a synthesis between the little things and the big things of life, a mystic marriage between the static self-contained community with which he was familiar in his immediate surroundings, and the rapidly growing, rapidly changing, cities and corporations from which he had fled, because they devoured men like the leviathan, subjecting them to an obscene process which reduced flesh and blood and brains and the unique individual qualities of men into an ever more bloated mass of undifferentiated blubber.

In one humorous passage he described himself as Jonah crawling inside the monster's stomach with a torch in his hand, exploring the mechanism by which men were digested and degraded, but in the end, he predicted, it was not the whale which would spew out Jonah, but Jonah who would spew out the whale.

Mrs Pat took the notebooks round to Macdougal, who poured over them uncomprehendingly for a whole winter. He had no glimmer of understanding of the Hobo's purpose, but he compiled a long list of the unusual words in the poem, identifying those which were archaic Gaelic and worth recording, and those which the poet had fashioned for himself like bridges to carry his thought into territory hitherto unexplored, although Macdougal did not understand that that was their purpose, dismissing them as bastard and inadmissible, debasing the purity of Gaelic speech.

"I've squeezed the lemon dry," he said, when he had finished. "There's nothing left of value for anyone else to extract."

Being a parsimonious man, he used the blank backs of the Hobo's pages for a weekly letter on current affairs he contributed to the local paper. The editor looked incuriously at the Gaelic verses scribbled on the other side, which had been scored out in red in Macdougal's schoolmasterish hand. He made some comment on Macdougal's meanness and thought no more about it. The evanescent weekly article in Macdougal's precise but stodgy prose was set in type and published and, when that had been accomplished, the manuscript, and with it the Hobo's poem, was consigned, sheet by sheet, to oblivion.

Macdougal, however, retained one of the Hobo's poems, because he thought he understood it, and it appealed to a side of his personality which was carefully screened from the public.

To him, it was a piece of rollicking bawdry describing a rape, and nothing more. The deeper meaning eluded him.

He did not keep the original. He was afraid there might be germs on the Hobo's notebook, so he copied it out in his own flowing style, and threw the original on the fire. The copy was carefully concealed where he could read it covertly when he felt inclined without the risk of anyone else in the household stumbling on it.

The existence of the poem remained unknown for many years until it came to light on Macdougal's death, and then it created a great sensation. That such a poem should be found in the library of a man of desiccated rectitude was surprising enough, but that he should have composed it, let

148

alone have got himself involved in the disreputable, but obviously real, incident which is described, was almost beyond belief.

Almost, but not quite. It was too tempting a morsel of gossip to let slip, and many a blameless elderly lady's reputation was smirched as the people of Seahaven strove to recall the past, and identify Macdougal's victim.

6

Fiddler in Hell

I walked up to the door. In fact, I got so far as ringing the bell. I heard it jangling away in the remote kitchen at the back of the house. I could see it in my mind's eye, for I had often watched it as a child, fascinated by the suddenness with which it started into life with no visible cause. A black iron bell-shaped bell—the pleonasm tells us something about the way language develops, although I don't know precisely what—on a black coiled spring which went on vibrating long after the sound had ceased.

There was something symbolic about the bell. It was so archaic, an apparatus of creaking wires and swivels through which an unseen hand controlled the actions, and to some extent the thoughts, of distant servitors. The whole house was archaic with its squat, projecting entrance, too pretentious for a porch, too insignificant and ill-proportioned for a portico, which emphasised the dull, heavy, threatening appearance of the whole frontage, bearing down on the spirit like a lowering sky.

I decided abruptly that I could not face the house at that moment. Or my father, although I had come to Geocrab specially to see him, because I knew that he was ill. I got the news in a roundabout way when someone I had bumped into casually asked me if he was making a good recovery, and I had to fumble for a suitably ambiguous answer because that was the first inkling I had had that anything was wrong.

"I will find out quietly in the village how things are," I told myself, "and go round in the morning armed with knowledge which will show that I keep in closer touch with them than they do with me."

"That'll wipe the bloody smile from his smug old face," I thought, moving swiftly from the doorstep to the shelter of the old rhododendron bush in which I had so often hidden as a child when I played a prank on my nursemaid, Lizzie, by ringing the bell and pouncing out on her when she stood in the doorway, looking up and down in astonishment at seeing no one there, although all the time she knew I was hiding, and was bracing herself to appear suitably startled by my sudden shout.

Lizzie was dead long ago, and it was my mother herself who came to the door. She had aged and shrivelled, and she seemed not so much surprised as terrified when she looked out and saw that there was no one there. "Don't tell me the old cow is superstitious in spite of her religion," I whispered. "I believe she sees it as an omen."

She slammed the door, and I could hear the bolt rattling home: a heavy iron bolt on a chain which would have held the anchor of a ship. "If she thinks she'll keep the ghosts out with a bolt and chain she's bloody well mistaken," I told myself—but deep down I knew that I was the haunted one.

What a mess I had made of my homecoming. I loved my mother with a love forged in childhood when her affection was extravagant because I was her last hope, my two elder brothers having died in infancy; it permeated my being so

151

completely that in moments of remorse I could feel it as a physical ache even in the dead and senseless parts like my very toenails. And yet I hated her more bitterly than I hated my father.

He was always himself—arrogant, blinkered, tyrannical but unequivocal; the same dye ran through the whole of the fabric, neither bleached nor faded, in fact time intensified it. He was an integer. If you chipped pieces off, you would diminish but you would not change him.

My mother, however, had betrayed her own love for me, her race, her language and her culture when she sided with him and began the long process of persuading me into courses I was determined not to take—an unremitting, quiet, remorseless pressure, sometimes completely silent, but more bruising than the thumbscrews, more agonising than the rack, more merciless than the Inquisition, and all the more intolerable because it was so patently unselfish, and might indeed be right. If she had been my ally I might have synthesised their qualities; I might have achieved the integrity my father had, with the understanding he so conspicuously lacked. Instead, I inherited my father's brittle narrowness and, taking up the cause my mother had renounced, became his mirror image, identical except that my posture in regard to the things that divided us was completely reversed.

I knew from a very early age that I could only assert my freedom by rebellion. I could not qualify my father's creed: I had to hate it. But I did not realise then, nor even on the night I turned away from my father's house and sickbed how completely I had become the same sad inflexible scarecrow, wearing a different suit of rags.

152

God, how I longed for a drink as I turned away from the house and hurried towards the village. "It is not the first time she slammed the door in my face," I complained to the darkness, making a grievance of my own boorish prank. In self-justification I brooded over all the occasions on which she had sided with my father against me. In particular, when she forbade me to spend my summer holidays with my grandmother, her own mother, in case I was defiled or corrupted. The peat smoke in the old black house at Carbost was bad for my lungs, she argued, to say nothing of the dirt left everywhere by the hens, the cattle, and the sheep. I might catch fever or pneumonia or consumption. No doubt there was an element of truth in it. Swaddled and protected as I was, I might have developed less resistance than my cousins, but it was not very long before I realised that it was not typhoid or T.B. my mother, in compliance with my father's prompting, feared, but Gaelic.

He was determined that I would be a schoolmaster, as he was: a classicist, and a musician. But he was equally determined that I would not waste myself, as he believed he was doing, in a Hebridean backwater, where he had gone originally only because his first wife was an alcoholic, a brilliant pianist in her lucid moments but so offensive when she was drunk that she had to be hidden away; and where he was irretrievably anchored when she fell from her bicycle in a drunken stupor, breaking her neck, and he married a local woman to care for the three daughters of the first marriage.

I was very fond of my half-sisters, and they doted on me, but in the school playground I never acknowledged them. They stood out from all the other children in their dress, their genteel avoidance of muddy patches and rough games, and more particularly in their language: always English, always polite, in contrast to the muddy barefoot oafs who raged around at every break playing football with a ball of paper or a cork, or shinty with rough, hewn boughs for camans, yelling vociferously at each other in Gaelic, unless they saw my father within earshot when they suddenly became dumb, or spoke in strangulated English whispers.

The use of Gaelic was forbidden within the boundaries of the school, including the playground, and I suspected that my sisters acted as my father's spies, when his wrath would fall like thunder from a clear sky on some unsuspecting boy who was hauled to the front of the class and belted viciously for no obvious or explained offence and sent back to his seat with raw palms and an aching sense of injustice which was only equalled by his stoic resolution not to admit the pain or the resentment even by the flicker of an eyelid.

My sisters formed an enclave in the school, a little society of their own, like an iridescent bead of oil refusing to mix with the common water round about, but I was a loner anxious to be absorbed. Besides, unlike my sisters, I could speak the language of my classmates. Lizzie used nothing but Gaelic when we were alone together, and my mother's stock of babying endearments was also restricted to Gaelic. She was fluent in English and a voracious reader but when it came to the real intimacies of life she reverted to the language of her own childhood.

Am I reading the prejudices of my adult life into my recollections when I visualise her cowering over my bed as she sang me to sleep in Gaelic, frightened that she might be overheard? Am I dreaming dreams I never really had when I recall myself wakening with a nightmare start to hear raised voices from the lower room as if they were quarrelling?

I cannot be sure, but I do know that my one aim as a boy was to identify in the playground with my peers, to keep my sister at arm's length, and to use Gaelic defiantly even in my father's hearing, a bit of *braggadocio* which I always regretted because he had no favourites and I got my thrashing with the rest. I refused to wear the clothes my mother chose for me. I must have corduroy knickerbockers like the other boys, worn with the knee buttons open so that they hung untidily about the calves, and a great scooped bonnet, as big and flat as a frying-pan on my tiny head, with a willow withy round the brim to keep it taut. And at night I often gathered with the group outside our own sitting-room window, listening for the moment when my father would take out his violin and begin to play so that we could all miaow in mockery of a sound which we despised because it was new to us. At least, it was new to the others. On the wet nights, when I had perforce to stay indoors, I often lay on the bedroom floor with my ear to the boards, listening avidly to the music of the great composers but without then learning their names or the identity of the pieces played, because I would not give my father the advantage over me of knowing my interest. I could ask no questions and had to nurse my love in secret. For the other boys our cats' chorus outside the window was a meaningless ploy. There was an element of hostility to the alien sounds, as I have said, a little of the vandalism that lurks in all of us when confronted with the disturbingly unfamiliar, but it was unimportant: the real urge was to thumb the nose at authority, to goad my father into chasing us with his belt, to enjoy the poacher's thrill of disappearing into the dark and watching the pursuit go blindly past. It was different for me. On these occasions I was denying myself to identify with them, just as my mother had denied herself to identify with my father, and my participation in the mocking of his music was a ritual of initiation which I performed with all the fury of the apostate. It was not a ploy but a crusade in which I had to prove myself before my comrades. I have sometimes wondered since whether they, although they did not show it, sensed my predicament and laughed at me as they laughed at my father.

Some of these ideas jostled each other in my mind that night as I turned away from home and left my mother on the doorstep wondering whether it was the ghost of her dying husband or her errant son which had disturbed her by creating the illusion that the doorbell had been rung, but only some of them, because the realisation of my own true state came at a later stage after my meeting with the Witch of Endor, as I lovingly call her, and the tinker who sent me to see her at the bottom of the pit.

It was purely by chance I met the tinker: one of the luckier chances of my life. I quickly decided as I walked away from the door that, thirsty though I was, I dare not venture into the village inn without exciting curiosity and even scandal. Besides, I had no wish at that moment to meet the men I had known as boys and be reminded of things which were already beginning subconsciously to trouble me. I carried on into the town, four miles away, cursing myself for turning back from the door with my visit unaccomplished, and trying to decide in which of the many Seahaven pubs I was least likely to meet a fellow villager or an acquaintance of my father who would ask embarrassing questions. I finally decided to go to Quay House, a tumble-down building on the waterfront patronised by English trawl-hands quarrelling in the accents of Lancashire or Humberside, foreign seamen whose Norwegian, Swedish or even Polish was hardly less incomprehensible to an islander than the English fishermen's English, and by local Seahaven dockers who quarrelled with equal ferocity and enriched their abuse with swear-words from both their tongues.

When I opened the door the smoke which met me was thicker than that of a kipper house, but it lacked the aromatic fragrance of the oak chips. Black twist, cheap cigars, navy cut cigarettes, the fumes of rum and whisky inhaled into the lungs of half a hundred drunks, and then exhaled in a babble of excited argument produced a fug which clutched the throat like a hangman's rope.

I would have drawn back but for the tinker, sitting on the edge of a table, playing the fiddle as if he were demented but failing, because of the din, to produce a single audible note. An overturned glass of beer lapped round his buttocks like a flowing tide, but he paid not the slightest attention to it, nor did he seem to be aware of the two dockers quarrel-ling over who had spilt it, or the barman struggling to separate them and throw them out. The table was rocked and his arm was jostled in the mêlée but he fiddled on regardless, the sweat pouring from his brow with the vigour of his bowing.

When the barman grappled with one of the dockers and frogmarched him to the door, there was a sudden silence, sharp like a clap of thunder, as the drinkers turned to look, and suddenly for a few precious seconds the music reached me. The tune was quite unknown to me, but it was unmistakably traditional and unmistakably old. Very old. There was something a little flat and tuneless about it at variance with the vigour of the playing, but it aroused my collector's curiosity and I determined that I must have it if it was the last thing I did. The martial erectness of the tinker's posture sitting on the sodden table, the intense concentration of his playing, gave me a vision of a court of kings where the tune might have been heard when it was new, but the dark skin, the dirty tousled hair, the ragged coat, and the faraway look in the eye suggested that its origins might be even older, in some pagan ritual dance of immense antiquity.

I made my way to the bar and got a bottle of whisky which I stuffed in my poacher's pocket, and then I got two large tots of trawler rum. I downed one where I stood and took the other to the tinker. He looked at it, winked and went on playing. I stood the glass on the table beside him, and waited for the tune to end, When it did, he emptied the glass so quickly it was back on the table before I saw him lift it. I bought him another and then said to him, "Come outside. I want you to play that tune again where I can hear it."

He grumbled about the cold so I gave him still another drink, although I had no wish to make him drunk as that might well defeat my purpose. At last I coaxed him out on to the pier. The black, tarred decking was white with hoar frost, the cloud had cleared and the moon was riding high above the harbour; it was brighter out of doors than in the murk of the public house, and the fresh sea air flushed out our smoke-filled lungs. The tinker sat on a wooden bollard while I squatted on a coil of rope, and so began one of the strangest recitals I have ever listened to. Strathspeys and reels danced and sparkled from his bowstring like the hoar frost in the moonlight, sad Gaelic songs stole across the harbour, soft as a lover's sigh, fragments of pibroch, the tunes of well-known ballads, Scots as well as Gaelic, and then incongruously, a modern dance. Everything but what I wanted most to hear. "I'll play it for you now, boy," he would say in reply to my entreaty, and start up something entirely different. Or he would look puzzled and say, "I don't know what you mean, boy." He even went so far as to deny that he had played that night in any public house. "No, boy, I wouldn't be seen dead in there," he said, indicating the Quay House bar from which we had both just come.

At last in desperation I said to him, "I'm coming home with you tonight; I have a bottle here to finish." I wondered how he would take the suggestion. I also wondered how I would fare if he took me at my word. I had collected many songs from tinkers in the past but I had hitherto drawn the line at visiting them in their own homes, although I was sometimes encouraged to do so. There is a strange freemasonry among folk musicians, especially the bearers of an old tradition forced underground by misunderstanding or contempt, and the collector is often referred by one musician to another for a version of a well-loved tune although sometimes, having regard to their place in society, it is difficult to imagine what commerce there could have been between the two.

"Come on, boy," he said at last, rising from the bollard and, without looking to see whether I was following he left the pier and strode out of Seahaven by the hill road towards an old gravel pit beside a little burn where there had been a tinkers' encampment at certain seasons of the year as far back as I can remember.

He left the road, such as it was, long before we reached the encampment, and cut across the open moor. It was certainly shorter and he took the bogs and peat banks in his stride, but I had difficulty in seeing them even with the aid of the moon, let alone avoiding them, and I was wet and muddy and uncomfortable long before we reached the sanctuary of the tent.

"Easy, boy, easy! It's not a night for swimming," he said to me when I made a bigger than ordinary splash, but he didn't slacken his pace or turn his head and I had to go ploughtering on because I was determined not to lose him. Then we came on to drier ground on a rising bank, and quite suddenly I was at the edge of the quarry looking down on a group of black beehive tents hugging the ground like giant snails.

I had been familiar with tinkers' tents from the outside as far back as I can remember and had often seen them being erected—a sheet of dark brown tarpaulin stretched over a framework of wooden hoops, primitive but brilliantly functional, the basic minimum required to throw off the Hebridean rain and offering not the slightest finger-hold to the ravenous Hebridean wind—but I had never been in one before, and I had a strange, almost superstitious, fear as I bent low and half crawled through the doorway, as if I were going to participate in some sinister black magic ritual, or perhaps was being led captive into a dark medieval dungeon from which there was no escape. Once inside, I found myself

160

surrounded by a friendly family warmth, although I could not see a thing.

The tinker was not troubled by the dark, and spoke by name to people I could not see but whom I soon began to recognise, at least as to their age and sex, by the voices replying, sometimes from so close at hand that I was startled. It was a darkness peopled by a wife and children greeting their father on his late return, relieved no doubt to find him reasonably sober, puzzled, surprised and delighted by the unexpected guest. They were bantering, inquisitive, talkative, with the younger children, as children inevitably do, competing for the attention of the father and his friend.

After a time, I was able to see that there was a little iron stove in the centre of the tent with an iron chimney thrust a few inches through the roof. There was a warmth through the tent which my wet and weary limbs found grateful and a not unpleasant smell of peat smoke which I am sure must have helped to deaden other human smells which would have been much less bearable in so confined a space.

When I stumbled in the darkness and made as if to catch the chimney for support, he quickly intercepted me, probably because he was afraid I might burn my hand on the hot chimney, but it may have been that he was afraid the chimney would not bear my weight. His comment was revealing. "These damn women, they will have stoves!" I demurred. The stove was an improvement on the open fire, I suggested gently, pointing out that there must be few travelling families who were so progressive.

"Progressive?" he said. "I don't know progressive, boy, but that damned stove makes a hole in the roof." I could see what he was at. The stove might be progress in that it got rid of the all-pervasive smoke, although not the smell of peat, but it breached the design of the tent, giving access to both wind and rain. There was no real resting place between a tent with an open hearth and a house which was beyond their means. We always pay for our aspirations.

He steadied me and guided me to the front of the stove which he opened, letting a little patch of light into the centre of the tent, although it failed to penetrate the dark shadows at the periphery, and I could still only vaguely discern the faces of the women and children huddled all around.

He made a seat for me of three or four large flat peats, and I wondered whose they were. The tinkers never stayed in one place long enough to cut and cure their own, even if they had the right to do so, and they were notorious but tolerated pilferers.

When we were seated in reasonable comfort and had warmed ourselves once or twice from my bottle, I explained to him as carefully as I could my purpose and my predicament. I had heard him play a tune, I said, which was a very old and beautiful tune. It was too precious to be lost. I had not heard it right through, and even if I had, I would have to hear it several times so that I could record it in the notation I had worked out for myself to cope with the grace notes of the old Gaelic songs which had defeated many earlier collectors with the result that wild, spontaneous idiosyncratic airs became bland or sickly-sweet in transcription.

When I think of the ease with which songs are recorded nowadays, I have difficulty even in recalling the labour I went through in my pioneering efforts when there was nothing to rely on but the ear, the memory and the notebook. A great deal has been saved, at least in part, by the efforts of collectors like the Kennedy Frasers, genuinely moved by love, but my passion went deeper, based as it was on hate, and the desire to expiate my father's crime. There was no limit to what I would sacrifice to save a genuine fragment from oblivion. The hardships and privations I suffered in these years were only tolerable because I knew my father suffered more from knowing how my time was occupied.

I had a long discussion that night with the tinker. It was not an argument because we were friendly throughout, but it developed into a sort of tug of war, because he was most reluctant to give me what I wanted, and when at last he was on the point of agreeing, his wife—or so I took her to be, although in appearance she could have been his mother, so early do the tinker women age, though in youth they can be dazzlingly beautiful—chimed in from the background and urged him to resist. I could not follow their conversation completely. They were bilingual like myself and switched at random from Gaelic into English and back again, but in both languages they had usages and pronunciations which completely baffled me. I did gather, however, that his wife had some superstitious objection to my taking down the song in my notebook. She seemed to fear it would give me some power over them. The song was as free as the birds, she said, when her husband whistled it or even when he played it on the fiddle, but who could tell what might happen to it or even to them if once I had it hidden in my pocket?

In the end of the day, as far as I could make out, it was his wife's attempts at dissuasion, becoming more and more voluble as she shared my whisky, that eventually won him over to my side. He had to assert his masculine authority and he did it with a magisterial command: "Whist, woman! Stop meddling in the business of men and make me a mug of tea."

She went away grumbling to get water from the river and, while she was out, the tinker told me, "Well, boy, it's like this. I cannot give you what I haven't got. I went to hell for that tune, down into the bottom of the bottomless pit. Down and down and down until I came to a little house where there was no one but a skinny old woman. She was that thin, at times I thought she wasn't there. And perhaps she wasn't. She may have been the Devil's mother for all I know, or the Devil himself in disguise, but anyway she put a spell on me and it's on me yet. I asked her for the tune because I knew she had it. That's what sent me there to begin with. She played it for me on a fiddle of her own, over and over again, and my heart was full of it. It's the strangest tune you ever heard with angels and devils singing to each other in a hundred different tongues, high shrill voices like I never heard before. When I thought I had it, she gave me the fiddle and I played it myself. I got it right enough, boy, the very first time, and I felt like a king as I played it. The sound was like precious stones dribbling out of my hand. I played it three times over and then I thanked her, and I gave her a flask of whisky I had with me because she seemed a poor lonely woman, and that's where I made the mistake. Once she had something of mine in her hand she put a spell on me, and it's working on me still. I've tried a hundred times to play that tune but the fiddle won't do it. I have the notes right, boy, and the time, but the tune

164

won't sing for me. It's not the tune I played that night in the devil's kitchen.

"That's the God's truth," he said. "I would give it to you if I had it. But I haven't. And it won't go away from me. Every minute of the day I can hear it in my head, and my hands are fingering the notes in my sleep. It's a spell, right enough, boy. To drive me out of my mind. And you know, boy, it's doing it. I play it out on the moor when there's no one to listen, and I try it in the pub where there's that much noise no one can hear it but myself. But, damn it, it's like an eel, you think you have it by the tail and it's that slippery you can't even see it going. If you want it, you'll have to go to hell yourself. I can't help you."

I had difficulty at first in making up my mind whether the tinker's hell was a real place which he so designated for some personal reasons of his own or whether it was purely allegorical. I wondered whether he had dreamt the tune up himself and was merely describing in exaggerated language the pangs of composition, which were in fact still continuing, because he was still dissatisfied with it. Although the tune was unfamiliar to me, I could understand what he meant: it was like seeing something brilliantly beautiful through a haze or a distorting mirror. Tentatively I asked him, "Is it a hard road to this hell of yours?"

"Bloody hard," he replied. "I thought my feet were in the butcher's mincer. My boots weren't much to begin with, but I had to throw them away. Then I wore my feet out till I was walking on the bloody bones."

I knew then that hell was real: he was talking about some place which was particularly difficult of access or where he had an unpleasant experience, or both. I passed the whisky round again and let him brood a while. Then we drank strong sweet tea. It was as black as a Highland river where water off a peat moor is lying still in a fathomless pool, and almost as thick as porridge, or so it seems in retrospect although I know that is impossible, but it was warm and, as it was a long time since I had eaten, my stomach was grateful.

"He's a fool with that fiddle," said his wife suddenly out of a long silence. "If he mended pans we would not be hungry so often."

"Shut up, woman," he said roughly. "You know as well as I do the tinker's trade is finished. It's the fiddle that keeps us alive." As if goaded by his wife's complaint, he reached for the instrument and played without further prompting the tune I heard in the pub.

I felt more determined than ever to get it then, and to get it from the source, but every time I broached the subject he shied away. He pretended that he was anxious to protect me from the spell which had been cast on him, but I knew it was just the musician's jealousy: he did not want me to win the prize which had so narrowly eluded him.

I turned my attention to his wife and began to ask her about the life of the travelling folk, in particular the up-bringing and education of the children who, like everyone else, were obliged by law to go to school, although what they learned there was even more remote from their needs and condition than for the average island child. The result was that after a guerrilla war with the Compulsory Officer, which lasted from the day they were due to go to school to their eventual release, they escaped from the hand of authority with scarcely a trace of formal schooling on the threadbare remnants of their own oral tradition which their schooling was designed to displace, although it still clothed their minds in a ragged sort of way. From that, I went on to ask her about the various villages she camped in, and the comparative attractions of the locations in regard to water, a dry floor, the accessibility of peats, and the chance of earning a penny begging from door to door, collecting rags, and occasionally, very occasionally, selling the odd drinking mug made from a Lyle's syrup tin with a handle soldered on: a sad decline from the ancient craftsmanship in gold and silver which made the tinkers a race apart and set them first on their still unended wandering.

"We have our places," she said, in the course of a long, rambling conversation, "but sometimes they put the dogs on us, and sometimes the police. I have stood before the law with my own father in the big prison in the town. There was a man there on a high seat like the king himself, with curly grey hair and a black robe. He had a great nose like a puffin, and little black eyes like a rat watching from his hole for the moment to bite. And my father had tears in his eyes. I was too frightened myself to cry. And my father was pleading with him to leave us on the pitch we had chosen because we were always there in the winter, and he had three sons serving the King in the war that was on then, and that was the only address he had for them to tell him were his sons alive or dead. But they wouldn't listen and my father had to pay them money out of his old black purse. And it was months before the letters reached us, wandering here and there. Each time they came in a little yellow envelope, and I had to go to the schoolmaster wherever we were, the first time and the second time and the third time,

167

and the schoolmaster told me that my brothers were dead and I had to go back and tell my mother and my father and the little ones that were too young to understand and went on playing their games as if it was just the same as any other day."

She was silent for a long time and I had the feeling that she was still weeping for the brothers she had lost all those years ago in the mud of Flanders, although I don't suppose she had any idea where or how or why it had happened. Then suddenly she looked up and said to me, "They were real men, not fiddling fools like that, wandering off to all the furtherest corners of the land where there's neither work nor money nor food, just fools like himself who sit up all night long screeching like cats as if you could fill the belly with noise."

She looked quickly to make sure that he was still too busy with his fiddling to hear her, and then she added, "He tried once to take me to Deepdale but I wouldn't go and he nearly didn't come back himself. I had to nurse him for weeks, lying there on his bed complaining of his feet and his back and God knows what. And since then he's been like a man demented. Either a woman or an evil spirit put a spell on him, for sure. There's nothing in his mind now but going back there and yet he's scared to go."

I said nothing and asked no more. Deepdale was the clue I wanted. I had never been there. It was nearly fifty miles from Geocrab, the last part of the route across a trackless moor. The most isolated village in the Hebrides. I had often heard of it but did not know for certain whether it was still inhabited. I made up my mind that I would set off first thing in the morning and catch my song if it was still alive.

It would be time enough to see my father when I got back, and I would face him more easily if I had such a rare talisman tucked away in my notebook and my memory, although it was not an achievement he would understand.

Soon after daybreak, I went into Seahaven to get a wash, collect my bag and look for a bus that would take me to the end of the Deepdale road, and that was quite an adventure in itself. The buses came into Seahaven from the rural villages in the morning and left for home in the evening, but their movements bore the same complicated relationship to the clock as do the tides which have their own regularity and rhythm but can only be pinned down to a precise hour by an elaborate calculation which requires a knowledge of the phases of the moon, the aberrations induced by irregularities of the local coastline, and which even then must make allowances for a sudden tempest which urges the water on or holds it back.

The island buses had not by that date been bureaucratised and subdued to a timetable. They left home when it suited the convenience of the driver and the most laggardly of the passengers. They halted here and there, as other buses do, to pick up passengers or set them down, but the halts were liable to be prolonged while the driver or some of his passengers got out to gossip with a bystander who had probably taken up a vantage point some time before at which the bus might stop, so that he could obtain news of a friend who was ill, or a couple getting married, or even learn the result of a football match or ask about the communion services in a remote parish he planned to visit if the officiating ministers included one of his favourites. In the town itself, the buses had no regular stops: they took their passengers where they wanted to go and picked them up again wherever the driver and the individual passengers agreed would be convenient. The period between arrival and departure was fully occupied as the bus moved from shop to shop and the driver fulfilled his major function as man of business for the whole community, buying a bottle of cough mixture from one chemist, a box of liver pills from another, according to their speciality, for there was still some individuality left in commerce; delivering a box of lobsters to a dealer who would miscount them if the driver let him get away with it, because he knew the Billingsgate firm to which he would consign them would, in turn, swear that half of them were dead on arrival even if they were still sprightly enough to dance a reel or bite a finger off: doubling back to buy a few fathoms of rope from a ship chandler's to tether someone's cow, and another few fathoms for someone else's boat: collecting a bag of yarn from the spinning mill for a weaver: delivering a consignment of pullovers or hose from a knitter: buying, as the orders came haphazardly back into his mind, a tin of waterglass for preserving eggs, a pail of sheep dip, a box of margarine, or a spade, and dumping them equally haphazardly in the bus, or so it would appear to the casual observer, although they were really stowed with a seaman's eye for the risk of shifting cargo on the rolling island roads, and with some regard for the order in which the different items would be delivered on the journey home. The buses themselves were built by local joiners on the chassis of a Ford or Chevrolet lorry, and the architecture was as varied as the goods they carried. Some were little better than a hen-shed on wheels, while others were put together with a loving craftsmanship and care more

170

appropriate to a vessel which had to contend with the open Atlantic in a winter hurricane than any land-based vehicle. Whatever their shape or size or colour, the buses were indispensable to the life of the villages they served, but at the same time they were, as I now realise, the vehicles of fundamental change, undermining, or at any rate, transforming, the social structure of the island I was trying to embalm, more effectively even than my father with his conscious purpose and missionary enthusiasm, which excused, and even sanctified for his employers, and perhaps even for his victims, the sadistic bullying with which he attempted to recreate the whole community in his own image, or at least such parts of his image as he thought appropriate.

I had the opportunity of surveying practically the whole island fleet of buses before I found the one I wanted. In fact, I missed it narrowly once or twice when I had to hurry down a close, or dive into a shop door, to avoid an acquaintance of my father who would ask me all the questions I most wished to avoid, questions not only about my father's health which I could not answer, but about my own prolonged absence from the island, for which I could offer no explanation they would regard as satisfactory or even begin to understand.

Eventually my arrangements were made. Big Neil, the bus driver from Carbost, who had been a lumberjack in Canada before he came home at the end of the First World War and bought a bus, made a rendezvous to pick me up when he was ready to leave town, and set me down at the Deepdale road end.

"You'll be going to see Anna Cas Bheag," was his comment as soon as I explained what I wanted. I agreed, although I did not know for sure, but the nickname sounded as if it might describe the sort of person I was looking for. 'Cas bheag' is the term the crofters use to describe their method of restraining a dog prone to chase the sheep, by tieing up one foot so that he must limp along on three. I have heard a Gaelic-speaking bus driver apply the same term to the use of low gear to supplement the brakes on a dangerous hill. It conjured up for me a picture of an aged hag hobbling about on a stick, which seemed to tally well enough with the tinker's witch. More importantly than these speculations, I realised for the first time, when I spoke to Big Neil, that I would have to make the seven-mile journey across the moor to Deepdale in the dark. It was an appalling prospect. The moor was notorious for sloughs and treacherous bogs and, as one approached the coast where Deepdale lay there was the Seal's Chimney, an unfenced circular hole so wide and deep you could drop a lighthouse down and never see it, and at the foot, so I had been told, a subterranean passage opened to the sea and you could hear the swish of unseen waves even on the calmest day. I had always wanted to see the Chimney but I had no ambition to stumble into it in the dark. The problem, however, had no sooner formed in my mind than it was resolved.

"There won't be a speck of moon tonight," said Big Neil, looking at the sombre clouds bellying in from the west. "You'll never make it. Stay the night with me in Carbost and I'll drop you off tomorrow on my way to town. Like that, you'll be able to do it in daylight, and I'll pick you up again tomorrow night."

I accepted his hospitality. In the morning, I set off across the moor to Deepdale in a smirr of rain. The distant mountains had disappeared, the moor was as grey and amorphous as the sky, there was no landmark, no feature, no horizon even, just an all-pervasive wetness into which I felt I was disappearing from my own sight.

"You'll have to be careful," Neil told me, having failed in his attempt to dissuade me altogether. "There's a rough track for about a mile. Then you come to a loch. Go round it to the right. Against the sun! I hope you're not superstitious. You better not be, because there's no other way. And don't lose sight of the loch, whatever you do, until you come to a little cairn of stones just above the bank. If you're lucky, you may find a flask of whisky hidden at the foot of the cairn. If you do, take a good dram, you'll need it before you reach Deepdale. From the cairn, you'll see the first of the marker stones the postman has set up to guide himself across the moor in weather like this. Go straight to it, and don't move from one stone until you've spotted the next. If it gets thicker and you can't see the next, stick beside the one you're at.

"That way," he added, with a smile, "we'll get your bones at least when the hoodies are done with you.

"Either stay the night with Anna, or get back here well before dark. You'll never make it otherwise. I'll be here as soon after nightfall as I can. If you're not here when I'm passing tonight, I'll look out for you again tomorrow."

"What about the Seal's Chimney?" I asked.

"The postman's markers will take you clear of that—if you stick to them. If you fall down it, it will be the end of you—and your own bloody fault."

With that, he put the car into gear and pulled away with

a great roar and clatter of gravel while I pursued myself into the murk, thinking how odd it was that, having at last braced myself to visit my ailing father, I had wandered off instead after an elusive song in the one part of Gaelic-speaking Scotland where I had not been able to collect over the previous twenty years, just because it was my native island and had associations I was struggling to break, although in every way it was the place I could have expected the easiest and probably the most plentiful harvest of the material I was looking for.

I reached the loch in due course, and the cairn. Nearby was a group of ancient beehive huts which I examined before looking for the postman's flask, as I guessed it must be. I found it and took a deep pull. By this time, I was sodden through but there was no point in turning back because there would be no transport until the evening. I had committed myself and, much as I had begun to regret it, I had to see the business through.

It was eerie, walking mile after mile through nothingness: a three-dimensional desert without shape or form, a void and a mirage, completely shapeless yet rolling into all the shapes the imagination could conceive, the mist boiling up around me in a perpetual act of creation, in which all the thoughts which had ever lodged in my mind appeared before me visible, concrete, startlingly clear, but illusory and evanescent. "No wonder the tinker thought it was haunted," I told myself, pressing on from one marker to the next, where I would pause, as I had at the last, to make sure that I could see another, fixed and durable even if vaguely seen amid the surrounding phantoms. Apart from the splashing of my feet on the sodden moor there was no sound of any sort. It

174

was not just an absence of noise, but the feeling that I was completely enclosed in some impervious substance noise could not penetrate, as if I were cocooned in foam rubber or polystyrene which excluded the living universe, although of course I did not think of it in these terms at the time because neither foam rubber nor polystyrene, certainly not the latter, had then been invented.

Having walked for many miles through the never-ending prison wall, pausing only to eat the salmon and chicken sandwiches the busman's wife had given me, I came on a larger cairn, and there I knew I must look for the start of another path, the descent into Deepdale, the notorious Scratch, so called, I had been told, because it looked from the other side of the bay like a nail mark, a thin line of broken skin, on the face of the precipice, which fell nearly a thousand feet sheer to the sea. I knew, too, from the cairn, that, half a mile back, where I had felt the ground begin to rise, I must have passed between the Seal's Chimney and the cliff edge, on the arch of rock which covered the underground passage.

The rain stopped just as I reached the Scratch, a fresh breeze from the sea was dispersing the last traces of the mist, and I found myself suddenly standing on the cliff top with the path tumbling down from my feet. Seabirds were crying eerily as they wheeled hundreds of feet below me. The last few wisps of the rapidly dispersing mist looked like steam rising from some evil potion boiling in a vast cauldron from whose rim I was looking down, dizzy and afraid "Down and down and down" the tinker had said. I knew now why he thought he had been to hell and back.

There was worse to come. The main path—such as it

was—led to the village, which consisted of a small cluster of thatched houses, most of them abandoned and ruinous, at the head of a long fiord, but Anna's house stood by itself in a secluded corner near the entrance. To reach it, one had to leave the path about halfway down and scramble diagonally across the steeply sloping face, dislodging scree which avalanched and thundered however carefully one moved. Her local visitors, her mail, and her household goods bypassed the direct route and came by way of the village where they might lie for an hour or two, or even a day or two, until a friendly fisherman found time to row with them several miles to her doorstep. My timetable did not permit that sort of margin.

Anna's father had been a gamekeeper. His house was strategically placed to watch the estuary to a world-famous salmon river. The river was now protected by a motor-boat travelling from the distant lodge, and the estate no longer kept a watcher at Deepdale. Anna and her father had, however, been permitted to stay on, rent free, and she had continued to do so, even after her father's death.

To me, as I came to understand the position during the three days I spent with her, it was almost as if she had taken up residence in her father's tomb. The house was isolated enough to be a burden on an active man in the prime of his manhood, with a family around to support him. It was utterly impossible for an ageing woman, alone, and growing daily less able to cope. Apart from the friendly fishermen at the head of the loch and the postman who kept her in some sort of touch with the outside world, she was almost as lonely as Robinson Crusoe on her little green peninsula, cut off by these frightening cliffs.

176

When I first glimpsed the tiny croft, it glowed like an emerald. The sea was grey and the rocks were grey but the grass shone after the rain, and I wondered by what freak of geology this little patch of fertile ground could exist between the bastion of rocks and the encroaching sea. It was almost as if some insignificant little state had established a zone of safety and of sanity between two warring empires and had succeeded in maintaining it against all probability.

Then I saw Anna herself, feeding her hens. She was scattering handfuls of mash, left and right, and the hens were so eager they were flapping up to peck the food almost before it left her hand. From the cliff face above, it looked as if she were stirring a whirlwind of squawking feathers. As I had expected, she was bent almost double with rheumatism, and had a heavy limp, the cas bheag of her nickname.

When she caught sight of me, she showed not the slightest surprise. She bade me welcome as naturally as if she had visitors every hour of the day, and as warmly as if I were a lifelong friend.

"You're wet," she said to me, in Gaelic. "Come in and get some dry clothes on."

She led me into a simple but comfortable kitchen. Being estate property, it was not thatched like the fishermen's cottages, and there was a fireplace in the gable end, which rather surprised me, because at that time most of the crofters' houses in the remote villages still had the fire in the middle of the floor with no chimney apart from a small vent in the roof. She took a pair of bellows from the hearth and vigorously fanned the peat into life. There was a teapot standing on the hob as if waiting for me, although I realised it was always there, when she poured out for me a thick black brew, stronger even than the tinker's, and which was only palatable because of the immense quantity of sugar she added to it.

"Strip off everything," she said. "And don't mind me. If you blush when you catch me looking, it will help to warm you up."

As she spoke her eye lit up merrily and, for a moment, behind the wrinkled face and the dark skin permanently stained by peat smoke and roughened by exposure to the weather, I caught the fleeting memory of a young, fresh, beautiful, carefree girl.

"How does one keep a sense of fun alive in a wilderness like this?" I asked myself. I had always thought of humour as a social accomplishment which must be freely exercised to survive. I could not help contrasting the placidity of this solitary woman, condemned to a lingering death in the prison of her circumstances, with my own bitter tensions.

My thoughts were interrupted by her return with a rough towel and what was obviously a suit of her dead father's tweeds. I rubbed myself vigorously and a great glow of comfort spread through my weary limbs as I dressed again.

"I will light a fire in the bedroom. It may be damp," she said, bustling off with an armful of peats.

"Look," I said, "I'm just here for the day. I don't need a bedroom."

"Be quiet with you," she said, hurrying out again with a glowing peat held in heavy iron tongs.

When she returned, she lifted one of my feet into her lap and looked at it quizzically. "If you could see your own blisters the way I can see them, you would be wondering

178

whether it's days or weeks you're going to spend with me. Your feet are in a bonny mess."

Unlike the tinker, I had been shod with strong walking boots, but I knew my feet were in a bad way, and I could imagine what his had been like when he discarded his worn-out remnants and finished the journey barefoot.

"They don't come courting me the way they used to do," she said gaily. "The last boy friend I had here was a tinker, and I had to bandage him up: his feet were like a lump of raw meat. If it wasn't for the smell, I would have kissed them, I was sorry for him."

It was perfectly natural that she should refer to a previous arrival whose plight had been similar to my own, but I had an uneasy feeling that she had actually read my thoughts. The feeling was reinforced when she said quite unexpectedly, "You've met the tinker. You've spent an evening with him!"

I was too astonished to say 'yes' or 'no', although since then I have persuaded myself that there is a simple explanation. Her reference to the tinker must have set me humming the tune which meant so much to both of us, and she would have recognised it even if I did not have it absolutely right.

"You'll have your dinner first. You can take salt herring?" I assented. "Then perhaps in the evening, when it's dark and cosy, I'll give you what you have come for."

If she had been younger or less crippled, her way of putting it might have been ambiguous, and even as it was, again as if reading my thoughts, she added with a smile, "I know fine what you have come for. Put your mind at rest: I don't think it is what you think I might think it is."

My biggest surprise came as she bustled about preparing the meal, and I was free to explore the little room. On the

179

rough wooden mantelpiece which seemed to be held in place by faith rather than anything physical, there was a photograph of a fine young man in academic robes.

"My brother, Donald," she said, before I had asked the question. "But he's not as good-looking as that today. Not as young, anyway."

She opened a drawer in the plain deal kitchen dresser and took out a number of snapshots. "There he is with Maureen and the family," she said.

Maureen had a bright intelligent face; she was simply but elegantly dressed, and she was standing with her children, two on each side of her, in front of an American wood-framed house, obviously located in a fair-sized garden or perhaps even in its own grounds.

"You'll have read some of his books," she said, indicating a row of formidable tomes standing on an old tea chest in a dark corner near the fire. "They're too deep for me. I never go beyond the Bible, and I don't quite understand why it wasn't sufficient for him as well."

I had seen none of the books before, although the names of one or two were vaguely familiar because I had read reviews in the local press, which had noticed them not because of the subject matter, on which the reviewer was obviously not qualified to comment, but because the author was a native of the island in whom, for some odd reason, his fellow-islanders were supposed necessarily to have an interest and indeed a sort of possessive pride, although he had obviously forgotten them—except his own immediate family—and perhaps repudiated them, because there is no record that he ever came back, even for the briefest visit.

"The Hollow Neigbourhood" was described by the publishers as "a study of the American dormitory suburb which is rapidly becoming a lifeless shell: an inhabited location which is not village or town or city because it has none of the attributes of a living community."

"Concentricity" was dubbed 'the onion book' by one of the specialist reviewers, because it peeled off layer by layer and anatomised the successive skins of social association in which a man is enclosed from his first realisation, lying in his mother's arms, that he is not alone in the world, through his discovery of village, parish and nation, until at last he understands that he is part of a world-wide community, and that his life only makes sense if it is related to the whole of mankind. "Members one of another" was the book's subtitle.

Looking back on them today, as I did recently to refresh my memory, the Biblical quotations give his books an archaic flavour. Many of our bright young sociologists would find the language off-putting, odd, stuffy, perhaps even offensive. At the time the books were written, however, they were ahead of their generation, and if they failed to make an impact outside the specialist field of sociology, where they were much squabbled over, it was because the world was not ready for them.

Some were straight academic text-books like "The Sociologist's Kit", a phrase book of specialist jargon, or rather an attempt to subordinate the chameleon words of everyday usage to the precise stability of a scientific vocabulary. Some were popular, and aimed at the mass, although they did not quite hit the target, like "Neither Beast nor God", with its Aristotlean overtones.

The book I read during my short stay with Anna, and

which disturbed me deeply, was called "The Chains We Forge", which was summarised on the dust-jacket as 'a tentative exploration of the processes by which ideas are conceived, crystalise and ossify; and a study of the factors in the development of the individual and the community which contribute to this process of degeneration. The author is troubled by the irony that those who are robust enough to break out of the intellectual carapace into which they are born do not escape into freedom but into a new captivity, a prison of their own devising'.

The book was dedicated to J. K. Finlay, 'who first raised my eyes to the far horizon'. Finlay had been an island headmaster for a number of years, like my father; in fact, they were close friends. Unlike my father, however, he had no compelling reason for remaining on his St Helena, and he moved on to become headmaster of a famous mainland school. He had not, so far as I know, become any more assimilated into the island community during his residence than my father, but he escaped before he became soured by isolation and the sense of failure. The dedication of that book by Donald Mackinnon must have been a great solace in his old age. My problem was to reconcile Mackinnon's magisterial command of the English language, the power and penetration and the reach of his mind, with the dead-end cottage where I found the books.

"Was your brother brought up in Deepdale?" I asked.

"I taught him his ABC," said Anna simply. "He was too sickly as a child to walk round the loch to the village school.

"We had a big school in those days," she added sadly. "Soon, all we'll need is a graveyard."

In a moment she was smiling again. "I made a good job of him, didn't I?" she asked, pointing to the books. "It gives me a funny feeling when I look at them as if I was the father of all these books and Donald the mother. He had all the bother of them but I started him off by giving him the ABC.

"When he was older and fitter he went to stay with an uncle and attended Mr Finlay's school," she continued. "When Mr Finlay left the island he took Donald with him to his new school. It was then we began to lose him." Again there was a little flicker of sadness, which never long survived her buoyant humour. 'Predestined serenity' was the phrase I coined for her prevailing mood. I had never before realised, although I was familiar with the phenomenon all my life, that the fatalism of the Gael makes for gloom only in some of its manifestations. It can also be the basis of an icy courage or a carefree acceptance of the passing moment as it comes, a humorous, self-deprecating realism, giving all and asking nothing, in which the purse, so to speak, is always empty and yet always full, because it is always being shared; a resolute acceptance of the human condition without illusions or regrets, which makes our modern intellectual stoics look trivial and perverted.

In the evening Anna opened an old sea chest in the room she had assigned to me and took out her fiddle.

Martin Martin records that there were many fiddlers in the Hebrides in his day, and as his dates correspond closely with the great flowering in Cremona when Stradivarius, the Amatis, and the Guarneris flourished, it would appear that the Gaeltacht was much more closely integrated into the ebb and flow of European mainstream culture before the Jacobite

Rebellion than has ever been accepted by the monoglot English establishment, which still holds to the view that it was they who rescued the Gaels from barbarism after voyages of exploration by Samuel Johnson and Walter Scott first brought their existence into the general consciousness of civilised people.

Despite the appearance of intellectual missionaries from the other side of the Gaelic curtain, or perhaps because of it, the fiddle has long ago been superseded by the accordion, a sad declension for anyone seriously interested in music, and even in Martin's day there is, so far as I know, no record of women fiddlers—although there were notable poetesses —and I was surprised to see Anna with the instrument tucked under her chin as naturally as if it were an extension of her own features and limbs, although it was precisely for that purpose I had come to Deepdale, and in the hope that she had saved something from Martin Martin's day, or even earlier.

At the first bar, I started forward in excitement. It was the tinker's tune, right enough, but how different! The music, which had been sluggish and flat as the tinker struggled with it, shimmered like the aurora which I used to watch as a child for hours on end from the garret window at Geocrab on a frosty night. More exciting than the music was the reason for the transformation. It was not in the playing but the tuning. Anna's fiddle was tuned to a pitch I had only heard once before, in a remote valley in the north of Norway. For a moment, I wondered whether the tune could possibly be a relic of the Viking occupation of the Hebrides, but that seemed impossible and, anyway, Anna disillusioned me.

"I got it from the only real lad I ever had," she said, when she had laid the fiddle aside. "I went to the fishing in Baltasound as a young girl. The foreman was a big, fair-haired Shetlander like the men from Ness in Lewis. An angel and a hero. I was ready to lie at his feet and let him use me as a doormat if he wanted. I think he would have done the same for me. . . . But, after that one season, I was never able to go back. I got the tune from him and I still play it for his sake. I always tune the fiddle the way he had it, and I never play anything else on it."

She looked into the peat fire in silence for a long time, and then she laughed. "I don't think I would have made a good Shetlander, in spite of the fiddle. It's here the good Lord meant me to die. But I'm glad I took the tune with me. He was no poorer for giving it, and I have been richer for getting it."

I was disappointed to find that the tinker's mysterious tune was such a late acquisition in the Hebrides, although how old it was in its Shetland and Norwegian provenance I could not guess. In any event, I did not regret my visit.

After she had laid the fiddle aside, Anna began to sing for me. She had a tremendous store of Gaelic songs, many of which I had never heard before or only in widely variant versions. On the second night, some of the fishermen from the village joined us and, after the ice was broken, they vied with each other in offering me long-forgotten gems, frequently struggling to retrieve from a fading memory words or cadences thrown into the rag-bag of disuse, which they were now surprised to find were valued by a stranger whose eccentricity they did not understand but were prepared to pander to, in accord with their tradition of hospitality.

Besides, one could sense a glimmer of pride and returning confidence as they realised that I regarded so highly what they had to give me of their very own. All the notebooks I had with me were filled by the time I set off hurriedly for home.

It was on the fourth morning, or rather early in the fourth afternoon, that a boat came across to Anna's from the village to tell me that my father was dead. No one in the family had sent me word, because no one who might have wanted to contact me had any idea where I was, but the busman from Carbost heard the news on his daily round in Seahaven and asked the postman to pass the information on to me as quickly as he could.

They did not send a messenger: every able-bodied man in the village came, led by the local missionary, or lay preacher, and they held a simple act of worship with me in Anna's kitchen before I set out on my journey—rather to my embarrassment, because it was sharply into my consciousness, and even my conscience, that I was more of a stranger in my own home than with these men whom I had known for only three days, in fact some of whom I was then meeting for the very first time.

When the service was over, they told me that the larger of the two fishing boats in which they came would take me to Seahaven, a distance of nearly forty nautical miles, so that I could get home more quickly than by the overland route to the once-daily bus.

I felt tempted to kiss Anna when I said goodbye, but the Gaels are undemonstrative, and I refrained. She held my hand for a long time. "Come back and see a lonely woman when you can," she said, and then, smiling sweetly, she

186

added, "It might save you from becoming a lonely old man.

"I was awakened the other morning by a hoodie crow," she added unexpectedly. "It was tap-tap-tapping at the window and me lying in my bed. To tell you the truth, I thought for a moment it was the Wicked One himself come to take me with him, and then I came to my senses and put on my clothes and went out to look. The hoodie flew off as I opened the door, but when I went across to the window I could see my own face in the glass. The silly thing had been pecking at his own reflection. I said to myself, 'It's a funny thing, but it's always two of a kind that fight'. I never saw two men squaring up to each other, or even getting into an argument but I thought how like they were to each other in everything except their looks."

She paused before she added, "The saddest thing of all is to see a man hating his own reflection in another man's eyes."

She turned back towards her little cottage, and I settled on board the fishing boat, wondering how far I had revealed myself to her in three short days. I also pondered on the fact that, although she spoke in simple Gaelic out of her own very circumscribed experience, while her brother wrote in erudite English coruscating with footnotes and quotations which displayed his familiarity with almost the whole field of human knowledge, the resonance was the same, and I was not quite sure that the simple wisdom did not bite deeper.

The fishermen respected my silence. Presumably, they thought I was absorbed in the family bereavement, although in truth I was wrestling with the discovery that hell is not a confrontation with the power of evil, but a casual encounter with someone better than oneself. Anna's profound innocence and, in a sense, purely worldly wisdom, brought me for the first time face to face with myself.

When at last I stepped ashore at Seahaven, and began to brace myself for the ordeal that lay ahead, I discovered that no power of argument or entreaty could persuade the fishermen to accept payment for the fuel they had used or the day's work they had lost. In fact, they stayed in Seahaven overnight and attended the funeral, as I saw, next day.

It was my youngest sister, Marie, who opened the door when I rang. We embraced with unusual warmth, I to hide my embarrassment and she because, as I discovered afterwards, they had been trying frantically to contact me through my city lodgings, and my various known acquaintances, because they were afraid that I would miss the funeral altogether and expose to the village how bitterly divided the family had become.

My oldest sister greeted me more icily. "Thank God you're keeping up appearances, at least," she said, but I soon realised that it was not so much my behaviour as my mother's that was troubling her.

There was not much opportunity for talk when I arrived. People were already gathering for the customary evening service, and even in the kitchen, where they took me for a bite of food, there were neighbours bustling about, many of them strangers to me because of my long absence.

Everyone present was wearing black, except myself. I arrived with nothing but the clothes I had been travelling in and, for the second time within a week, I suffered the indignity of wearing a dead man's suit: this time it was one of my father's who fortunately was much my own build. I thought it was the supreme irony, a practical joke by Anna's humorous, tolerant but deflating Deity, that I should walk behind the coffin of the man I hated wearing his own discarded clothes.

My sisters, although dressed in black, were still conspicuous. The city chic of their mourning separated them from the village matrons as sharply as Joseph's coat, or their English speech. My mother, however, was reabsorbed completely into the local background and not only in appearance. I was surprised to discover that, during my father's protracted illness, she had reverted gradually but totally, and had become what she might well have been if she had married one of the local fishermen instead of the intrusive, alien, abrasive schoolmaster. She was surrounded by all the relatives she had held at arm's length in my childhood, out of deference to my father's wish that I should be Anglicised, and it was obvious that they had not come (like me) in a last-minute effort to keep up appearances on a solemn occasion; the breach had been healed some time before, and they had all the stigmata of a victorious faction enjoying their triumph with ostentatious modesty.

The service was long and eloquent and emotional, and it was conducted exclusively in Gaelic. No concession was made to the three English-speaking daughters, the persons most deeply bereaved, hardly excepting the widow. On that day, they were more isolated in the home of their childhood than ever I had been, and for the first time in my life I felt deeply sorry for them.

They made no complaint. Outwardly, they seemed to accept my mother's decision to have an exclusively Gaelic service as being completely natural, although it was out of character with her own behaviour over the years, and grotesquely inappropriate, having regard to my father's lifelong stance. It was perhaps easier for them than it had been for me when our roles were reversed because I was then a child, whereas they knew that in a few days they would escape again to their employment in city schools and hospitals. I admired their forbearance and, before we parted, a few days after the funeral, I apologised to them for having failed to assert my authority as the only son and alter my mother's inconsiderate arrangements. They assured me it was the last thing they would have wished.

I stayed on in Geocrab with my mother when they had gone, but I found myself no more in sympathy with her new mood than I had been in the days of my rebellion, although I hope more tolerant. We came closest to quarrelling over the question of my father's tombstone. With a perversity worthy of myself she wished to have the inscription, like the funeral service, in Gaelic, and with even less excuse. Not many island families in those days could afford tombstones but those who could had the inscription invariably in English. I had often thought it absurd that people who had loved and planned and quarrelled and prayed and mourned in Gaelic should be commemorated in English, as if that was the only tongue the Almighty could understand, but at least one could say that it was logical in that the schools had taught them to read in English but many were still illiterate in their mother tongue. It was a greater absurdity than the only monoglot Anglophile in the graveyard should lie beneath a Gaelic slab, commemorated by an inscription he could not have read himself if he were still alive, and none of his family could read now that he was dead, apart from the son who had repudiated him and had shunned him even on his death bed.

I reasoned with my mother as gently as I could without success and then, in a happy moment, I suggested to her that so notable a classicist should be commemorated in Latin. She readily agreed because that was an aspect of her husband's achievement she could admire without reservation since it was neutral and had not contributed to the quarrels which had separated her for so long, first from her brothers and sisters, and then from her son.

Incorporated in the design are three short bars of music, an unusual feature which still evokes the interest of visitors to the ancient Culdee ruins in the corner of the graveyard who stumble casually on my father's tombstone. My mother believed until her death, although I never said so explicitly, that the music was from one of my father's favourite violin concertos. In truth, it is from something he never heard, and would not have appreciated if he had, but it is the secret sign of my compact with myself to cherish the memory of the old woman who taught me that no individual, community or culture can live to itself, even in an isolated cottage miles from the nearest inhabited place. The human spirit lives by giving and borrowing.

When, in the days following the funeral, I took stock of my own position, I found that the motive which had driven me to lead a Spartan life in pursuit of songs for my collection had disappeared. Hate had been the mainspring, but that hatred was dead. I still believed—and do even to this day—that the work I had done was well worth doing, and that future generations would look on my collection with gratitude and indeed with a certain awe. I was saddened, however, by the realisation that I had done a right thing for a wrong reason, but consoled myself with the knowledge that in this imperfect world the right thing will not often be done otherwise.

After much brooding, I decided that the time had come to put into service the qualifications I had acquired under my father's goading, but had not hitherto used. I applied for the post made vacant by his death and, because of my strong family connections, I was able, a little shamefacedly, to get it, despite my lack of practical teaching experience.

That was many years ago, and now that I have come to the stage of retiring, I feel it is proper to set on record some of the almost forgotten events which shaped my course during a teaching career which, I hope, rendered a greater service to the cause of education in the sense of cultural reconciliation and enrichment than was perhaps recognised by successive school inspectors, applying their own necessary but, in both senses of the term, highly discriminating slide rule.